RIDERS OF THE SUNDOWNS

RIDERS OF THE SUNDOWNS

Wayne D. Overholser

GUNSMOKE

This hardback edition 2010
by BBC Audiobooks Ltd
by arrangement with
Golden West Literary Agency

ISBN 978 1 408 46310 9

An earlier condensed version of this story appeared under the
title "Riders of Carne Cove" in *West Magazine* (1/47).

British Library Cataloguing in Publication Data available.

Printed and bound in Great Britain by
CPI Antony Rowe, Chippenham and Eastbourne

RIDERS OF THE SUNDOWNS

Chapter One

Mack Jarvis came out of his feed store and into the street, pausing there in the spring sunlight while the restlessness in him boiled until the ferment was in his mind. It had been this way all through the months since he had quit riding for Tomahawk and had bought the feed store here in Axehandle. He never should have done it. He had known it then as well as he knew it now, but he had set himself to do two things — one of which would make the other possible. He could have done neither if he had stayed with Tomahawk.

"Mack," Deputy Natty Gordon called. "Lou's setting 'em up in the Casino. He wants everybody over there. Says he's got a couple of things to tell us."

The little deputy ran on along the boardwalk without waiting for Mack's answer. It was like Gordon, Mack thought, to be running errands for Lou Kyle. Too, it was like Kyle to send out word he had something to say and expect everybody to light out on a high lope to hear it. What was more, they would. All but Mack Jarvis. He could wait and hear what Kyle had to tell second hand.

Mack slanted across the street to the Top Notch Café, stamped the dust from his boots, and went in. He said: "Howdy, Betty," swung a long leg over a stool, and sat down.

"Steak and onions?" Betty Grant asked. She watched him, smiling a little and hiding behind that smile the knowledge she had of him. "If it is, I won't cook it. It's a waste of my culinary artistry the way you douse it with ketchup."

"A cup of coffee," Mack said soberly.

"Might be you've lost your appetite." She observed this as she poured the coffee and set the cup before him. "What's the

7

matter with Natty Gordon?"

"He was running another one of Lou Kyle's important errands. We're all supposed to trot over to the Casino and hear something Kyle's got to say."

"I thought so." Betty pushed the sugar bowl toward Mack. "He wouldn't hurry that fast if it was a matter of enforcing the law. He'd probably be going the other way." She watched Mack spoon sugar into his coffee. "You going?"

"I didn't figger I would," Mack said sourly. "I reckon I ought to . . . the way I'm sitting between a rock and a hard place with Kyle, owning the bank, and the bank, holding a mortgage on my store building, and me not in shape to pay that mortgage. It's just that I don't have any hankering to hear him blow off."

For a time Mack sat, stirring his coffee, staring unseeingly at the pies on the shelf behind the counter. His life had been a wild dream thrown down a rough and rocky channel. More than a year ago he had quit Tomahawk and put every cent he had saved or could borrow into his feed store. He hated it. He hated everything about it. He hated the bookkeeping. He hated being inside. Still, knowing that, he had made his choice. It was to have been the means of gaining the thing he wanted most. He sat with his long legs bent behind him, gray eyes narrowing as he looked back along his twenty-seven years, saw the one bright spot in his life, and saw in that same glance the shadows fencing it in.

Inky Blair came in then, hoisted his heavy body onto the stool beside Mack, and said loudly: "Peach pie, Betty. Another slab for the skinny gent to my left. Got to get some meat on his bones, or they'll be coming through."

"The skinny gent says he isn't hungry." Betty slipped a quarter of a pie onto a plate and slid it along the counter to Inky.

"Not hungry?" Inky scratched his bald spot. "He's sick. I'll get the doc."

"Eat your pie," Mack growled. "Put a cup of sugar on it. Betty, you oughta charge this *hombre* twice for pie. He's getting double the sugar . . . and for free."

Inky sprinkled three dripping spoonfuls of sugar over his pie wedge. "Don't give the lady ideas, my lad. She might do it, and at this moment the Axehandle *Weekly Times* is not prosperous enough to pay for my sugar."

"Funny thing," Mack mused, "how money and power get all twisted up."

"You changed the subject fast." Inky shoved the sugar bowl back.

"Take Lou Kyle for instance," Mack went on. "He's got the stageline, does all the freighting into Axehandle, owns the bank and the Mercantile, and all in a mighty short space of time."

"He didn't have much when he came in here. Mack, sometimes I wonder if that yahoo has as much money as he pretends."

"Looks like he's got enough. He just waggles his little finger, and we're supposed to come running."

Inky jabbed his fork into the last morsel of pie. "Mighty good, lady. You'll make some man a fine wife long as you can turn out pies like this." Inky slid off the stool. "Come on, Mack. Let's go hear what Kyle's got to say. Betty, that pie . . . just put it on my tab."

"I don't reckon I'll go." Mack laid a coin on the counter. "I'll read about it in the *Times*. Betty, don't keep on handing out meals to this keg of lard. He'll bust you sure."

"Don't call me a keg of lard." Inky shook a pudgy finger under Mack's nose. "Likewise, it isn't good politics to pass up one of Kyle's invitations."

"Why not on both counts?" Mack demanded. "You sure are a keg of lard, and I don't give a damn about Lou Kyle and his politics."

"Look, son," Inky said, suddenly serious, "it never pays to buck a man when he holds four aces."

"It might be Kyle has something to say that concerns you, Mack," Betty said. "You're the one man who doesn't bow and scrape around in front of him."

"Come on." Inky had moved to the door. "Reckon they're all there but us."

Here was something Mack couldn't put his hands on. It wasn't like Betty to be worried, as she was, nor was Inky often deadly serious as he was now. It was as if a shadow had fallen across Mack's path, and from where he stood he could not see the substance that gave that shadow form.

"I sure hate to give Kyle the satisfaction of knowing I jump to any tune he whistles," Mack said as reluctantly he followed Inky into the street. He laid a gaze across his friend's rotund face. "You and Betty seem to know something I don't, like mebbe what Kyle's gonna say."

"So help me, son, I don't know," Inky blurted. "That is, I'm not sure. I just figure you ought to be there. I might be bothered over nothing, but I've got a hunch this is the day you decide one way or the other."

"What are you gabbing about?"

"You'll soon know. We haven't got time to augur now."

They had arrived at the Casino. Inky put a shoulder to the batwings and went in, Mack behind him.

There were a dozen men in the Casino, forming a line at the bar. Lou Kyle was in the middle, a blocky, black-eyed man driven by a great ambition that would never let him stop, short of death. In the year Mack had operated the feed store, he had learned that Kyle was not a man to drive hard at the thing he sought. Rather he would take a wide and circuitous route that promised the greatest success and the least risk. He was, Mack judged, both a schemer and a killer, and therefore a doubly dangerous enemy. An expression of malicious triumph crossed Kyle's face when he saw who had come in, triumph mingled with the shrewd cunning that was always there in his dark eyes.

"All right, gents," Kyle called loudly, his words stopping the run of talk along the bar. "Looks like we're all here. Step up, Jarvis, and you, Blair. This is my day to howl, so drink the Casino dry if you're man enough to do it. We're taking two rounds because I've got two important things to say."

"Spit her out, Lou," Natty Gordon yelled. "We're behind you."

"All right, all right." Kyle grinned and motioned to the barman. "Put her down, boys, and then bend your ears this way."

Deputy Natty Gordon was like the rest — a fawning bunch of lame-brained, spineless fools who stood around like a pack of hungry hounds with their mouths open, waiting for whatever juicy morsel Lou Kyle felt like tossing them. That was the way Mack saw them. He left his drink on the bar, the sourness washing through him, and he was thinking that the only one here who could be called half a man was Inky Blair.

Kyle had stepped away from the bar and stood, facing the townsmen, his eyes covertly on Mack. It struck Mack then that what Kyle was going to say would affect him mightily. The whole play, he was thinking, was rigged for his benefit.

"I'll make the less important announcement first," Kyle said. "In view of Axehandle's recent growth and prospects of future growth, I have decided to go into the feed business. It will be run in connection with the Mercantile."

A dozen pairs of eyes whipped to Mack and came back to Kyle. It was exactly what Mack should have expected. Lou

Kyle was a showoff. He wouldn't take the ordinary way of using the bank to close Mack out. He'd start a competitive business, and, because he had the money to stock varieties and large amounts of feed, he'd have a better store than Mack could ever have. More than that, folks would buy from him because they'd be afraid to buy anywhere else.

"Have you noticed Axehandle's recent growth, Inky?" Mack asked out of the corner of his mouth.

Inky shook his head and said nothing. He was watching Kyle who, like an egotistical actor, was squeezing the last clap of applause from his audience. They were giving him what he wanted — slapping him on the back, shaking his hand, telling him loudly that he'd get their business. Only Mack and Inky kept their places at the bar.

Kyle was smiling and assuring his admirers they'd get the same good service he'd always given in the Mercantile. "This is just a starter," he glowed. "Here's the real one, and I don't mind saying I'm the luckiest gent who ever lived. Drink up. Make it double. This is the day I've been looking for, so the sky's the limit."

Mack should have seen it then. He caught Kyle's quick glance of triumph as the big man stepped to the bar and took his drink. There was only one thing that could make Lou Kyle so confident, but Mack didn't see it because it was the one thing he didn't believe would ever happen.

Mack left his drink untouched on the bar as Kyle moved back to face the townsmen. What he said struck Mack exactly the same as if Kyle had driven a cold, sharp knife into his middle.

"I am happy to announce my engagement to Miss Rosella Wade," Kyle said. "I know I have your wishes for my happiness. That is" — his eyes flicked to Mack again and came away — "from most of you."

12

There was a moment of silence then, silence broken only by men's gusty breathing and the shuffle of feet, silence that left Kyle, staring at the men along the bar, in puzzled uncertainty. All of them knew why Mack had left Tomahawk and bought the feed store. For a man to use his wealth and power to drive a competitor out of business was one thing, but to use that power to steal the girl a man loved was something else. It was too much even for these men habitually subservient to Lou Kyle's will.

In Mack there was a shocked stillness, a vacuum of thought and feeling in which life stopped, and there was no hope anywhere. Then it passed, and he was thinking: *He's done it this way for me. He wants me to break before everybody in town.*

A coldness ruled Mack then. However deep the hurt, Lou Kyle would not see the wound. It was Mack's voice that first broke the silence. He stepped toward Kyle, his face without expression. "I hope Rosella will be happy. Any man who has her love is to be congratulated."

"She recognized a good man when she saw one," Kyle taunted.

"You claim to be a good man, do you, Lou?" Mack asked softly.

"Good enough to rake the pot in from under *your* nose."

There was a crescent-shaped scar on Mack's right cheek that had come from a fist fight he'd had when he'd ridden for Tomahawk. In those days the solution to any problem had been simple. The easy ones could be cracked with a pair of fists, the tough ones with a gun. It was different now. The years had brought a cold and sober judgment, a self-control that kept his hands at his sides, but it was a self-control that was near the breaking point. Mack's right hand came up to his face, fingertips rubbing the crescent-shaped scar. It was a signal that rashness was crowding him, and Inky, recognizing

13

it, moved forward to stand beside Mack.

"Let's drift, son," Inky said. "We don't want any more of Kyle's rotgut."

From the bar Natty Gordon cried: "She'll sure make you a purty wife, Lou. When's it going to be?"

No one else along the bar voiced his congratulations. Mack didn't move, nor did Kyle answer Natty Gordon's question. They stood facing each other, tall, gray-eyed Mack Jarvis whose love for Rosella Wade went back over the years, and thick-bodied Lou Kyle who could offer Rosella everything that money could buy and wanted her because she was the prettiest girl in the Axehandle country.

There was silence again that ribboned on and on until it was unbearable. Those along the bar — and Inky Blair who kept his place beside Mack — could not guess what the next seconds might bring. The feeling between these two was not new. The issues were as old and fundamental as life itself, and the clash between them had been predestined by a willful fate that now was working out one of the tightest knots it had ever tangled into its twine.

Again it was Mack's voice that laid aside the silence. "Mebbe Rosella thought she saw a good man. I feel sorry for her if that's what she thinks. You're a little man, and you know it. This business is a pretty fair sample of it. You cooked up this party, thinking I'd crawl out of here like a worm on his belly. You got me plumb wrong, mister. I ain't crawling out of here for any little man."

At the back end of the bar a great bear of a man shook himself, shoved the empty sarsaparilla bottle back, and plodded toward Kyle, head down. He was Tash Terris, as great of muscle as he was small of brain. He was Kyle's man, body and soul, and he needed no great mind because Kyle did his thinking.

14

"You're talking like a big man," Kyle said, "which doesn't make you one. Personally I like Rosella's judgment."

"You would," Mack breathed.

Tash Terris was standing beside Kyle then, beady eyes honed to a sharp wickedness. He said: "Want I should give it to him now, Boss?"

"No need for trouble," Natty Gordon called from the bar. "You hear, Lou Kyle? And that means you too, Tash! No fighting in here."

Kyle smiled, but it was a smile that held neither mirth nor pleasure. This, Mack saw, was not going the way Kyle had planned it. Whether he had signaled Terris or not, Mack couldn't tell. In either case, Terris was here beside him, but still he hesitated. Kyle's eyes held the glitter of black frost. It was as if he wanted to see Mack smashed, but there was a natural caution that held him back. He jerked a thumb toward the end of the bar where Terris had been standing. "Go on, Tash. Git." Then his eyes came again to Mack. "I'll carry your good wishes to Rosella."

"Thanks." Mack wheeled toward the batwings and paused there. "Lou, it always seemed to me that a good man did his own fighting instead of hiring a gorilla to do the job. Whenever you feel like having a go at it personal, come around."

Mack did not wait for an answer. The batwings gave to his shoulder. He turned toward his feed store, walking fast, long lips tightly compressed. Inky ran beside him, his fat body shaking. Between puffs he asked: "See what I meant when I told you . . . you'd have to decide one way or the other?"

"Yeah, I see, and I've decided. I'm going to skin Lou Kyle and hang his hide on hell's outside door so it'll dry."

Chapter Two

There must be some reason for Kyle's suddenly wanting to go into the feed business. That thought was in Mack's mind as he made the turn into his store and strode past Dad Perrod into his living quarters at the back. Perrod worked for Mack at times, and he made — with Inky Blair and Betty Grant — the sum total of people in Axehandle Mack could call friends. Dad Perrod had a look at Mack's gray, strained face and hoisted himself up from the sack of wheat where he'd been sitting.

"What's the matter with the boy?" Perrod asked Inky.

"Got kicked in the chest by a mule," Inky answered and followed Mack into the back room, leaving Perrod, staring after him and muttering under his breath that he thought Mack had more sense than to get in front of the business end of a mule.

Mack was stuffing food into a flour sack when Inky came in. He glanced up and grinned crookedly. "I feel kind of like a man, coming out from under an anesthetic, after he's had his legs whacked off."

"I know how you feel." Inky leaned against a door casing, wanting to say something and not finding quite the right words.

"I doubt that like hell. Go tell Dad to get my horse out of the stable. Tell him to get a move on."

"Sure." Inky stepped back into the store. When he returned, he asked: "What do you reckon made Rosella tell that son of Satan she'd marry him?"

"It's her dad. Old Soogan loves Rosella and money. Nothing else." Mack knotted a string around the grub sack and tossed it on the bed. "That's why I bought the store, and a hell of a bad deal it was, but I didn't have enough to buy anything else, and I couldn't save enough out of the thirty a month I got

16

buckarooing for Soogan to ever make him think I was fit to be his son-in-law."

"Yeah, sure." Inky bobbed his head. "But I figured Rosella was all set to wait for you. You haven't told me why she isn't."

"It's Soogan, I told you." Mack reached for his gun belt, hanging from a nail on the wall. "For some reason she thinks a lot of that ornery old fellow, and he wants her hitched up to a lot of dollar signs before he cashes in. Reckon he made it so hot for her she gave in." Mack buckled the gun belt around him. "How'd you and Betty know what was up?"

"We just made a good guess," Inky answered soberly. "You've been so danged busy, trying to make this store pay, that you haven't had your eyes open. Kyle's been riding out to Tomahawk two, three times a week. Then Rosella was in town a few days ago and asked Betty to make her a wedding layout."

"Looks like they're fixing to get hitched right away." Mack stepped into the corner and came back with his Winchester.

"I dunno for sure." Inky nodded at the rifle. "What're you aiming to do with that?"

"Going hunting. Dad got that animal out there yet?"

Inky looked in the direction of the front door. "Don't see him." He looked back. "No sense in getting all busted up about this, Mack. Why you've been so crazy about Rosella and never could see Betty is more'n I know."

Mack sat down on the bed and rolled a smoke. "I've seen some gents make right big fools out of themselves over women. Reckon I'm not above it."

"I wish Betty thought about me like she does you," Inky said. "For my money she's the finest thing that ever put on a skirt."

"Betty don't think much of me. You've been writing too many editorials."

"Maybe." Inky jabbed a forefinger at the Winchester. "I still don't know what you're aiming to do. If you want to fill Kyle full of holes, you don't need a horse."

"I'd rather ventilate Kyle's hide than anything else I can think of," Mack said, "but this just ain't the time. I've been wondering why Kyle decided to go into the feed business."

"The railroad's the answer, if I'm guessing right. Most folks haven't guessed, but it seems to be more than just the talk we've been hearing. There's been several surveying parties along the right-of-way south of here, and it looks to me as if the grading might start in a few days."

"It takes a lot of horses to do the grading," Mack said thoughtfully.

Inky nodded. "It does for a fact. Now, I haven't heard that the company has made any official announcement, but a man told me yesterday he'd seen a lot of construction material piled up in Minter City."

"Kyle would know about that before anybody else around here would," Mack mused, "and, if he's gonna furnish the railroad camps with hay and grain, he's gonna need quite a pile."

"Maybe you'd better see the Carne boys since they're the only ones in these parts who sell hay."

"That's what I'm aiming to do."

Perrod came in then. "You gonna ride out to Carne Cove, Mack?"

"Yeah, thought I would."

"They'll plug you first and talk second," the old man warned. He stood pulling at his beard, faded eyes on Mack. "I wouldn't do it."

"I bought hay from 'em last year, Dad. I'll make out all right." Mack rose, put out his cigarette, and picked up his Winchester. "I'm likely to be gone for a day or two. Kyle says he's gonna have a crack at the feed business, so we'll have about as much chance of staying in the game as a man would have to bake a batch of biscuits in hell."

"If he shows his ugly face around here I'll dust him off with buckshot."

"Don't do that, Dad. Let him play his hand out. He might get rough, so if you want to lock up. . . ."

The old man flinched as if he'd been hurt. He said simply: "Mack, you oughta know me better'n that. I ain't made like these female men who kowtow around Kyle."

"Sorry, Dad." A crooked grin came to Mack's face. "Looks like I've got a friend or two."

"Yeah, for all the good they'll do." Perrod jerked a thumb at Inky. "You won't get much out of that keg of taller, and I'm too old to do much fighting."

"There's Jimmy Hinton out in the desert," Inky said, "but he spends too much time reading Shakespeare and Plato to do any good. Son, it strikes me you'd be smart to keep on riding."

"I ain't smart. So long."

Mack nodded and walked out. He mounted his sorrel gelding and took the high desert road out of Axehandle. When he reached the rim east of town, he reined up and looked down upon it. Axehandle was a pleasant place — made pleasant by the rows of trim poplars, the picket fences, the white houses with green shutters. The town was set alongside the swift water of Pioneer Creek where it broke out of the trench it had dug between the Sundown Mountains on the west and the high desert on the east. It held a sort of hominess, an air of stability, an unchanging quality as if the flow of time had been an even one.

Yet there was actually no real stability about the town. Lou Kyle's coming three years ago had destroyed that. In one way or another everybody in Axehandle made his living the way

Kyle willed it, and the extent of that living depended on how high a man stood in Kyle's good graces. He'd come first as the new owner of the stageline, operating between Axehandle and the Columbia River. He'd bought the freight outfits, then the Mercantile, and finally the bank. As to how much actual capital Lou Kyle had, no one in Axehandle knew, and Mack, thinking about it now, wondered if Kyle's sudden move into the feed business might have been prompted by a need for quick cash to keep his many enterprises going.

Mack turned in the saddle and stared across the valley. Held between rapidly widening walls of rimrock, Pioneer Valley was a patchwork of sagebrush and grain fields. Someday it would be cut into small, irrigated farms. That day would come when the government dammed Pioneer Creek above Axehandle and used the high walls of the cañon for a reservoir. Then a feed store in Axehandle would be a prosperous business, but it might be five years — perhaps ten — and Soogan Wade had not let Rosella wait.

Mack turned his sorrel and went on. Five miles from town he swung north, leaving the county road that would have taken him to Soogan Wade's Tomahawk, and followed the twin ruts that led to the cañon farm known as Carne Cove. Beyond the cove was Jimmy Hinton's homestead, just south of the Sundown Mountains that lay east of Pioneer Cañon. Because Hinton had filed on the one sizable spring in that entire northern half of the high desert, he had run afoul of Soogan Wade, but despite the old cowman's threats Hinton had hung on stubbornly.

Here, as on most of the bunchgrass range of eastern Oregon, water was life. There was a deep well at Soogan's home ranch and a few springs that were little more than seeps. Pioneer Creek flanked Tomahawk range, but only in one place did the east wall of the cañon break down to the water in a gradual slope so that cattle could go down to drink. It was because of this watering place that most of the Tomahawk cattle were held between the cañon and the ranch buildings, and the great bulk of the high desert grass went untouched year after year.

As Mack covered the ten miles between the county road and Carne Cove, his mind went back to Rosella Wade. A great emptiness came into him, a vacuum where a dream had been. Both of Mack's parents had died when he was six. From that time the years of his youth had held little that made for happy memories. There was work, and more work, and often too little to eat. An uncle and his sour-faced wife had taken Mack. Through those years, when he should have played and dreamed a boy's wild dreams, there had been a man's work to do. He'd run away when he was fourteen, drifted south to the border and then north to the Axehandle country in eastern Oregon, a tumbleweed who had found no fence to rest against until he'd signed on with Soogan Wade. Then he'd met Rosella, and he'd come to love her.

The first time Mack saw Rosella the vision had come to him, tall and wide and deep. It had stayed with him through the heat and the cold, the thirst and the hunger, the nights without sleep, and the soul-deep weariness that is a buckaroo's lot. It had stayed with him after he'd bought the feed store, a year that had been like a prison sentence. Now it was gone, leaving in him that strange emptiness which comes to a man when there seems no purpose in his living.

Mack reached the Carne gate and reined up, staring at it in profound amazement. Years ago old man Carne had blasted a narrow road out of the side of the cañon that gave a steep passage to the floor of the cove. He'd blocked the entrance with a gate of light juniper poles, letting his own evil reputation keep strangers away, but this gate was something else. It was made of pine logs that the Carne boys must have brought from

21

the Sundowns beyond Jimmy Hinton's homestead. The logs had been recently cut, for the sawed ends were not yet discolored by the spring rains. One end of the gate was hinged to a heavy post. The other end was chained and padlocked to a second post as heavy as the first. Even more surprising than the gate was the scrawled sign, tacked to the top log of the gate, the words spelled in the Carnes' own, original style:

NO INTRINSE
TU NOBODE
RODE DINIMITED
STA OUT

Mack swung down and walked to the gate. He put a palm against a post and found it as solid as it looked. This had been no easy job — and a senseless one, as far as Mack could see. He had never heard of anyone going into the cove outside of the Carnes themselves, except old Soogan Wade, and Soogan hadn't stayed long. The youngest boy, Cat, had escorted him out with a gun.

Wings had been built at both ends of the gate which extended at an angle to the sheer wall of the cliff. It was two hundred feet or more to the deep, fertile soil of the cove floor. For a time Mack stood beside the gate, smoking and trying vainly to think of some logical explanation for what the Carne brothers had done. Then anger rose in him. This was no way for honest men to live. He'd come on a business errand, and he didn't aim to go back until he'd contracted for the hay he needed.

Old man Carne had homesteaded the cove long before there had been an Axehandle. He'd raised three sons, flatly told folks to stay out of the cove, and they had taken him at his word. He'd died, and his wife had died, both without friends, and

22

his boys had followed the same aloof pattern of living, except that they did come to town occasionally to get blind, roaring drunk. It had been on such an occasion the previous summer that Mack had cornered the oldest boy, Dan, and arranged to buy fifty tons of hay. The Carnes had hauled the hay, Mack had paid them for it, and there had been no trouble, but this year he couldn't afford to wait until the Carne boys got thirsty.

Mack climbed to the middle log of the gate and leaned over the top to look down upon the Carne buildings. The log house was set hard against the cliff almost below the gate. There was a log barn, a number of smaller buildings, and two corrals. Three wagons with hayracks on them stood at the end of the barn. The alfalfa fields were green, and Mack guessed the first cutting would not be far distant.

Swearing softly, Mack got down and drew his gun. He could shoot the padlock off and ride down. It would serve the Carnes right. They had no business padlocking their gate. The whole thing smelled like owlhoot, a smell Mack recognized. There was a good chance the Carne boys were hiding outlaws in the cove and were frantic in their fear that their game might be discovered. If he'd guessed right, he'd get a hot reception when he got to the bottom, but that was a chance he'd take.

Mack stepped back, lining his gun on the padlock, but he didn't squeeze the trigger. A Winchester spoke from the jumble of lava to his right. The first bullet lifted his hat from his head; the second breathed by within inches of his cheek. Hard on the heels of the dying echoes of rifle fire came the flat-toned voice of Cat Carne. "Stick that iron back in leather, Jarvis. Then mount up and ride like the devil was sitting the saddle with you."

Chapter Three

The first wild impulse that rocketed across Mack's brain was to obey, to mount, dig in the steel, and make a run for it. Then the impulse passed. He dropped his gun into leather and slowly brought his hands above his head.

He called: "Come on out, Cat. I rode out here to talk to you boys."

For a moment there was no answer, a moment that strained Mack's nerves to the breaking point. Cat Carne was the youngest and most unpredictable of the unpredictable Carnes, a skinny, quick-tempered man with three killings to his credit in Axehandle that Mack knew about. It would be like him to go into a sudden rage, because Mack had not obeyed his orders, and shoot him down. Murder would be safe enough for the Carnes. Natty Gordon was not one to poke around in the cove to find a lonely grave with a bullet-riddled body in it.

But Cat Carne didn't shoot. He asked: "Whatta you want, Jarvis?"

"Come on out, Cat. I'll bust a lung hollering at you back there."

Again there was silence while young Carne turned it over in his mind. Then his gaunt body rose from its hiding place in the tumbled lava mass. He came toward Mack slowly, the cocked Winchester carried hip high, cold, green eyes not wavering from Mack's face. When he was ten feet away, he stopped and cuffed back his battered Stetson. His voice held a grudging admiration when he said: "You've got guts, Jarvis. Most *hombres* would of lit out of here so fast they'd have left their shadows standing by the gate."

"Thanks, Cat." Mack picked up his Stetson. "Long as we're

passing out compliments I don't mind giving you one. You've got quite a name around Axehandle for being a tough hand after you salivated that gambler last winter."

Carne's skinny face showed his pleasure. He said in a self-deprecatory tone: "Aw, hell, that wasn't anything. That jigger was just plumb slow. Why, I had time to blow my nose twice before I plugged him."

Mack shook his head. "Pretty fast job, I'd say." He jerked a thumb at the gate. "What's the idea of that, Cat? The last time I rode by here the old gate your dad put up was still there."

Carne's green eyes narrowed. "You got no call to ask questions, Jarvis. What the Carnes do is their business."

"That's right," Mack agreed. "Only thing is folks will talk. Might accuse you of things you don't do. I figgered if I knew the reason I could put 'em straight."

"We don't want no snooping. That's all. If anybody asks you, you tell 'em that. That old pole gate wouldn't hold nobody out."

"Nobody ever bothered you boys, did they?"

"You damned right we been bothered," Carne said savagely, "and we don't like it. Old Soogan Wade came plumb down to the house just to ask about some hay."

"That so?" Mack shook his head in disapproval. "That reminds me, Cat. I came out here to see about buying your hay this year. Might be able to use all you've got. Figgered I'd take the carryover to boot."

"Can't let you have none, Jarvis. We ain't even selling Wade none. He was plumb out, old Soogan was. Wouldn't surprise me to see him come snooping around again. He'll sure get drilled between the eyes if he does." He snickered. "Mebbe you'd like it if we did, Jarvis. I hear tell he won't let you marry his gal."

Mack shook his head. "I wouldn't want him beefed. He'll cash in soon enough from old age."

Carne snickered again. "I dunno why a man wants to have a danged female around, but that Wade gal is plumb purty for a fact. I hear she even nabbed Lou Kyle. Guess you kind of got kicked in the face."

"My bad luck." Mack's temper was crowding him, but he couldn't let it go. Not yet. It was queer that Cat Carne would know about Kyle's and Rosella's engagement. None of the Carnes had been in town for a month or more. It meant, then, that Lou Kyle had been out here, talking to them. So Mack asked, his voice carefully casual: "Is Kyle buying all your hay?"

"That's right." Carne nodded. "Paying us a dollar more a ton than you gave us last year."

"Do you reckon Kyle would let me have some?"

"You're sure gonna be plumb out, mister, 'cause Kyle won't let none go. No, sir! He'll sell all he can get from us to them railroad. . . ." Carne caught himself, a quick wave of red washing across his nervous face. His voice was coldly hostile when he said: "Git, Jarvis. Go on now. Don't snoop around no more, or by damn I'll drill you and talk afterwards. Git, I said."

Cat Carne was ready to kill. It was there in the shrill tension of his voice, in the sudden hardening of his green eyes. Mack Jarvis would gain nothing by staying but a bullet in his brain. He nodded, said: "So long, Cat," and mounted. He didn't look back as he rode away.

Disappointment was keen in Mack. He might have known Kyle would not give away his hand until he was certain where the big cards lay. The Jarvis Feed Store was done. Mack might as well ride back and pull down the sign. He still had a few tons of hay and some grain. That was all, and he couldn't afford to have more freighted in from The Dalles.

26

Inky Blair's guess as to why Kyle had gone into the feed business was confirmed by the slip Cat Carne had made, but the knowledge was of no great value. Mack could see little sense in seeking a market among the railroad construction camps when he had nothing to sell. He might still be able to pick up some grain and possibly a few tons of rye hay from the dry farmers in the valley below town, but there was no real hope in him. The chances were Kyle had been there ahead of him.

Mack had been riding aimlessly, letting his sorrel have his head, his thoughts on what he had learned from Cat Carne. Now he was aware that the shadows were long, and that he was headed squarely for Tomahawk's ranch house. Rosella would be there. He didn't want to see her. Not now. So Mack reined his horse westward to Buck Spring, and there made camp.

Buck Spring was ten miles or more from Pioneer Cañon and was the only water between the ranch and the creek, but the flow was small. There would be a day, if Soogan ever had the money to drill deep wells, when this range would support twice the number of cattle it did now, but deep wells were expensive. Such developments would be years ahead unless — and Mack swore fiercely at the thought — Lou Kyle had agreed to put up the money for those wells after his marriage to Rosella.

Mack built a fire and cooked supper. When he had finished, he stood up and gazed across the desert. He had ridden over this range hundreds of times when he was buckarooing for Tomahawk. Before dusk had come he had seen cattle grazing in the tall bunchgrass between him and the creek. Now, with the sun gone from the sky, there was no motion and no sound, only a great sweep of land belonging to Soogan Wade. That was Tomahawk, an empire which would go to Rosella when

27

Soogan died. In that way it would become Lou Kyle's.

Soogan had made Tomahawk by shoving and elbowing people out of his way exactly as Kyle was shoving Mack out of his way now, but there was a difference. Kyle had money when he came to Axehandle. Soogan had started from nothing, a thirty-a-month buckaroo who had ridden for a little outfit along the creek below Axehandle. He had moved out here on the desert and had started with a dozen cows under his iron. His herd had grown miraculously fast. Some said a wide loop had helped. Mack didn't know about that. In any case all the high desert was Tomahawk range now. The other outfits had gone. This Soogan had done for Rosella, or so he had told Mack. Her life was to be different from her mother's. If the money he left her didn't keep her in comfort, her husband's would.

Mack built up the fire and lay on his back, head on his saddle, eyes on the clear, far brightness of the stars, the thoughts in his mind the disturbed, bitter thoughts of a man who suddenly finds he has no anchor to hold him. He had been that way before he had met Rosella. Now there was nothing but a faint hope that a broken dream might be pieced together.

He heard the run of a horse, sat up, and listened. It was north of him, and he thought it was a Tomahawk hand riding back to the ranch. Then the sound was gone, and he relaxed. His thoughts, without conscious guidance, came again to Rosella. He forgot about the rider until, minutes later, he heard the horse coming through the junipers directly behind him.

With one quick swing of his foot Mack scattered the fire and spilled on over it into the sagebrush. He plucked his gun, turning back toward the still bright coals, and waited. Then relief washed through him, and he felt suddenly foolish. Rosella

Wade's voice came from the darkness, "Why did you kick the fire out, Mack?"

Mack slipped his gun back into his holster and rose. "Guess I'm a mite boogery." He scraped the coals together, and, as he piled on more sagebrush, Rosella rode close to the fire. When there was a flame again, he looked at her for a long moment, satisfying the deep hunger for the sight of her that had been in him.

Rosella sat motionless in the saddle, watching him closely, her hands folded over the horn. She was a tall and shapely girl who carried herself with uncommon grace. Now, coming in off the desert, dust lay in a thick, gray coat upon her riding skirt and green jacket, yet she was perfectly poised, thoroughly at ease, and utterly desirable. Honey gold hair curled under the brim of her Stetson. Her red lips held a small smile in their corners, a humor that was reflected in her blue eyes.

"This is like coming home, Mack," Rosella said softly.

"Reckon so."

"You haven't been out to see us for a long time," Rosella prodded.

Anger gave a sharpness to Mack's words. "Why in hell should I? It's Lou Kyle you've been wanting to see, isn't it?"

Her lips formed the word no, but she didn't say it. She sat a moment, watching him, holding her emotions under a tight discipline. Then she said: "So you've heard?"

Mack nodded. "Kyle got us together in the Casino so he could have the proper congratulations." Then the stiffness broke in Mack, and words, no longer dammed by self-control, rushed out of him. "Why did you do it, Rosella? I know Soogan's held up a dollar sign in front of your eyes ever since you were big enough to walk, but that wasn't enough to make you give Kyle your promise."

Her words came to him across a great distance. "Mack, did

it ever strike you that I might have made up my own mind?"

"No. I don't think you did. Soogan shoved you into Kyle's arms, and there'll be a day when he'll feel like shooting himself for doing it."

"Perhaps it's just as well you haven't been out to see us."

Mack gestured wearily. "I know what Lou Kyle is. Whatever you think of me, don't marry him." He would not beg her, would not let her know what she had done to him. She should have known. "Mebbe we can find something else to talk about like why I heard your horse going lickety-larrup for home, then didn't hear it, and next thing I knew you showed up right at my back."

"I was going home, but I saw your fire, and I wanted to see who was here. We've got trouble, Mack. I'm afraid of what may come of it. The boys are finishing the roundup, and we're short. I don't know how many, but a lot."

"Short?" Mack laughed lightly. "What kind of locoed talk is that? Soogan never had a beef stolen in his life. They couldn't be. Nowhere for 'em to go."

"That's just it. Dad says it's like having a ghost. . . ."

A gun roared from behind Mack, the bullet raising a geyser of sparks from the fire.

"Don't move," Rosella whispered. "We'll see who it is in a minute."

Slowly Mack's hands came up, and he was thinking again of Cat Carne. But it wasn't Carne's flat, hard voice that came to him from the junipers. It was Metolius Neele who said: "Keep 'em up, Jarvis. I'd kind of like to plug you. Rosella, light out for home."

Mack would have felt better if it had been Cat Carne. The feeling between him and Neele went back to the first day he'd ridden for Tomahawk. Slowly one hand dropped to his face, fingers rubbing the red, crescent-shaped scar. Neele's fist had

30

given him that scar. He'd licked Neele, the only time the man had ever taken a beating, and Neele was not one to forget. He'd waited a long time for this moment.

Chapter Four

Neele rode into the firelight, a cocked Colt held unwaveringly on Mack. He was a red-haired man with a pair of bright blue eyes that were constantly alert for trouble and a flat nose that had been liberally spread across his face by Mack's fist. His thin-lipped mouth held a sly smile, as if he had caught Rosella and Mack in some furtive act they had been carefully trying to conceal.

"I should have known you were following me," Rosella cried furiously. "I suppose Dad put you to playing nursemaid for me."

"Something like that," Neele agreed, his eyes pinned on Mack. "You go on now, Rosella. Reckon I'd better ride into town and tell Kyle about you two meeting out here where you figgered nobody would see you."

"I wouldn't do that." Mack edged away from where he had stood beside Rosella's horse. "What Kyle hears is gonna be what Rosella tells him."

"You ain't in no shape to tell me what'll happen, mister." Neele jerked a thumb in the direction of the Tomahawk ranch house and nodded at Rosella. "Soogan figgered you was up to something. Start riding, and mebbe I won't tell him what I seen. I'll tend to this yahoo myself."

"You haven't seen anything, and I'm not up to anything," Rosella said flatly. "What's more, I won't be tagged around like I was a six-year-old. I saw the light of his fire, and I thought it might be some of the rustlers, so I rode. . . ."

"Rustlers?" Neele bellowed. "That's it. Sure as hell's hot. That's what he's out here for. Why didn't I think of it sooner? All right, Jarvis. Where are them cows you stole?"

"Got 'em in my pocket. Wouldn't be no other place to keep 'em around here, would there?"

"Funny, ain't you?" Neele sneered. "If you're as smart as you are comical, you might have cooked up a nice scheme for getting rid of three hundred head. Or mebbe that nester friend of yours thought up something."

"Now mebbe Jimmy ran the cows in with his hogs, Metolius. He's got a nice bunch of hogs. Mebbe he fattened 'em on beef. They're all cannibals. The last time I was up there, Jimmy turned his hogs loose after a bear. You should have seen that bear travel. He went back into the Sundowns twenty miles with the hogs right on his tail, every one of 'em yapping like spotted hounds. Funniest dang hogs I ever did see."

"Yeah, you sure are funny." Neele shot a puzzled glance at Rosella, as if he didn't quite know how to get her started. "Guess I'll take you into town and turn you over to Natty Gordon. Kyle will enjoy seeing you sit in the calaboose for a spell."

Mack knew he would never get to town alive. He edged on around the fire, hoping for some kind of a break, and seeing little chance for one. Sooner or later Rosella would ride on, not knowing what was in Neele's mind. Then there would only be the question of when Neele would kill him.

"You haven't got anything to hold Mack on," Rosella said scornfully. "Just because I found him, sitting beside a fire on Tomahawk range, doesn't mean he's a rustler."

"You just happened to find him, did you?" Neele said mockingly. "Then what was he doing here?"

"That's none of your business." Mack lowered his hands several inches. "My arms are getting plumb tired. How about . . . ?"

"Keep 'em up," Neele snarled, his eyes again fixed on Mack.

"Either you're a cow thief, or you're out here to meet Lou Kyle's girl on the sly. Reckon Soogan or Kyle would say I done right if I beefed you on either count. I ain't one to cut down a man who ain't got a chance, so I'll take you to town. Throw your saddle on your sorrel and. . . ."

Rosella whirled her horse and put him hard at Neele's mount. The action came without warning, and the Tomahawk man was entirely unprepared. His horse spun, reared, and came close to piling him. When at last he had fought the animal back under control, he had lost his Colt and found himself looking into the black bore of Mack's gun.

Mack's voice came ominously to Neele. "Drop your Winchester alongside that hogleg, mister, and ride."

For a moment the man hesitated, hate a brightness in his eyes. Reluctantly he let his rifle go. He said to Rosella: "You're a she-devil. Before I'm done I'll square this with both of you." Then he rode away into the junipers.

"Thanks," Mack said. "My hide ain't worth much, but I'm obliged to you, Rosella, for keeping some holes out of it."

"Your hide is worth a great deal, Mack. Don't ever think anything else."

"If you really think so," he said roughly, "why did you give your word to Lou Kyle?"

For a moment he thought she was going to give him an answer. Then without a word she put her horse around, keeping the back of her head to him so that he could not see her face. She called over her shoulder: "You'd better kick out your fire again, and don't stay here in the morning." She was gone, the night and the junipers hiding her, and presently the sound of her horse's hoofs died. There was only silence then, save for the stomping of Mack's sorrel and the far cry of a coyote, a silence that stretched on into the night while the fire went out, and a great loneliness was in Mack Jarvis.

* * * * *

Before the starlight had died in the morning, Mack was in the saddle and riding southeast toward Pioneer Valley. He spent the morning and most of the afternoon riding from one farmhouse to another, but the answer to his question was always the same. There was neither grain nor hay to sell. Most of them needed every bushel and ton they had kept. Two said Kyle had bought all they could spare.

Mack was not surprised by what he learned. He was surprised by what the farmers said about the railroad. Every farmer swore lustily at himself for not having grain to sell, but the action of the Pioneer Valley Railroad Company had been swift and unexpected. The right of way had been bought years ago. More than one survey had been made, so, when another group of surveyors had come into the valley, nobody had thought much about it. Now they were thinking about it. Within a matter of hours opinion had changed. All the farmers were convinced that actual construction would begin in a few days.

"They tell me them surveyors are doing cross-section work," one man said, "so I reckon they're ready to start construction. Gonna be a lot of horses in here, shoving that dirt around. They'll be using plenty of hay and grain, and I sure wish I had some to sell."

Another farmer told Mack he had been down the creek to Minter City where he had seen piles of construction material. "It's what we've been waiting for, Jarvis. There ain't no doubt about it now. I saw wheelbarrows, tents, blankets, scrapers, them steel rods they use for rock drilling, and more danged horses than I ever saw in my life." He groaned and shook his head. "I sure wish I had a million sacks of oats and a million tons of hay to sell. I'll bet them critters eat that much before harvest."

It was a strange prank of fate, Mack thought somberly as he rode back to Axehandle. For a year he'd hung on to his feed store, making a poor living selling grain and hay to the Axehandle livery stable and the cowmen in the Sundowns, hog feed to Jimmy Hinton, and odds and ends to the dry land farmers and the townspeople. He'd hung on because he'd hoped something would happen that would give him the stake he needed to satisfy Soogan Wade. Now that something had happened, it was too late. Rosella was promised to Kyle, and he had nothing to sell.

Mack left his sorrel in the stable and found Dad Perrod alone in the store. He asked: "Any business, Dad?"

"Sure." Perrod drew a plug of tobacco and a knife from his pocket and sliced off a chew. He eyed Mack as he replaced the plug and volunteered no additional information.

"Well?"

"Well, what?" Perrod spat at a knothole in the floor and missed. "You know, Mack, since Doc pulled them last twenty-four teeth of mine, I just can't hit my hat if I hold it under my chin."

"You know damned well what I mean," Mack said angrily. "Dad, sometimes I think your head is nine-tenths bone and the other tenth just empty. I want to know what business we did while I was gone."

"Why, I took a sack of wheat over to Miss Peterson. Mack, that danged schoolmarm don't have no more business with chickens than the man in the moon. She eats the pullets, raises the roosters, and wonders why in hell she don't get no eggs. You reckon I oughta tell her, Mack?"

"No. Let her find out for herself. Is that all?"

"Why, I reckon it is. Can't seem to recollect nothing more." Perrod's brow furrowed in thought. "Well, now, come to think of it, there was one more thing that happened. Lou Kyle came in this morning with that overgrown quarter-brain he calls Tash

36

Terris and wanted to talk to you. When I says you ain't here, he wants to know where you were. He seemed to kind of have a notion you'd gone out to see Miss Rosella."

Mack grinned, wondering what Kyle would say when he heard what had happened the evening before. If he heard it from Metolius Neele, he'd have plenty to say.

"What'd he want?" Mack asked.

"I got the idea he wanted to buy you out." Perrod spat again at the knothole and cursed when he missed. He wiped his mouth with the back of a hair-tufted hand. "He said he'd be over to see you soon as you got back, and, by grab, there he is now. Speak about the devil, and you're sure bound to hear him come stomping in."

Mack moved away from Perrod and stood with his left side to the counter, right hand brushing his gun butt. He nodded and said: "Howdy, Kyle."

"Howdy, Jarvis." Kyle stood in the doorway, his blocky figure silhouetted there, his eyes making a quick survey of the store.

"Mebbe you'd like some hay for that mare of yours," Mack said, "seeing as you ain't got your store set up."

"I've got enough to get along," Kyle said.

"Hay's gonna be plumb short around here," Mack urged. "Some yahoo bought all the hay the Carne boys have and this year's crop to boot. You wouldn't want your mare to starve to death, Kyle. Mebbe this galoot that bought up the Carne hay wouldn't sell to you."

Kyle came in, his meaty-lipped mouth spread in a wide grin. "So you've been out to see the Carne boys, have you, Jarvis? Reckon you had the ride for nothing. I'm the gent that bought their hay, so my mare will get all she needs."

Tash Terris had come in behind Kyle, his beady eyes filled with dislike for Mack. Lou Kyle was a big man, but, standing now in front of Terris, he looked less than average size.

Mack jabbed a forefinger in Terris's direction. "Have you always got to have that gorilla with you, Kyle?"

"I like him," Kyle said placidly.

"Get him out of here," Mack snapped.

"He'll go with me in a minute." Kyle drew a cigar from his pocket. "You heard the news about the railroad coming this summer?"

Mack nodded. "A lot of equipment in Minter City, they tell me. The railroad will be a great thing for this country, Kyle. We won't have to pay you the tariff we've been paying. I'll be able to buy hay and have it shipped in, which will fix the Carne boys so they won't be in position to bargain like they are now."

Kyle bit off the end of the cigar. "Freight will be cheaper, of course. Whether you'll be around to buy hay is another matter." He felt in his pocket for a match, found none, and turned to Terris behind him. "Got a match, Tash?"

"Sure, Boss."

Mack said nothing until Terris had struck the match and held it to the end of Kyle's cigar. Then he said: "I'll bet that baboon dressed you, Kyle."

A muttered oath came from Terris's throat. He spread his hands, his heavy fingers splayed, slow anger bringing a dull red to his beefy face. He rumbled: "Boss, he called me a gorilla, and now he calls me a baboon. I don't like it." He clenched his fists and spread his fingers again. "Want I should give it to him now, Boss?"

"Shut up, Tash," Kyle said sharply. "Let's get down to business, Jarvis. The railroad means that this valley will boom. That's why I'm going into the feed business."

"There ain't much you've overlooked. Why don't you do a little bartering on the side? Or mebbe start a new harness shop?

How about another livery stable?"

Kyle tongued the cigar to the other side of his mouth. "I'm not here to be hoorawed, Jarvis. I aim to make you a fair proposition. I don't like competition. I can wait and let you starve, but I'd rather do it this way. I'll buy you out. One thousand dollars for everything the way she stands." He nodded at Perrod. "I'll even give the old man a job. He's not worth anything, but you don't pay him much, so it's a fair deal."

Perrod spat an amber stream at the knothole. "You know, Mack," he said contemptuously, "I've seen a lot of funny-looking crawling things, but that there ape back of Kyle sure does take the cake."

"Ape?" Terris rumbled. "I ain't no ape. I ain't gonna be called no ape. Boss, I'm gonna bust him."

Terris started toward Perrod and stopped only when Mack's gun appeared in his hand, the barrel lined on the giant's wide middle. "Get back, Terris, or I'll gut shoot you. The answer's no, Kyle."

Perrod cackled. "That's right, Mack. Long as we got a sack of chop to sell, let's keep her open."

"I'll give you two thousand," Kyle said coldly. "The only joker is that you leave the country as soon as you're paid. I don't want you around here, starting another store with my money."

"No." Mack watched Terris reluctantly draw back to his place behind Kyle. "Lou, it doesn't make sense for a nickel pincher like you to talk about two thousand dollars when you claim all you've got to do is to sit tight and let me starve."

"I told you I didn't like competition, but, if that's your choice, I'll get rid of you in one way or another. Make no mistake about that. Come on, Tash."

Kyle went out, a cloud of cigar smoke fouling the air behind him, Terris at his heels. When they were gone, Mack said somberly: "Dad, we're crazy. Both of us."

Perrod took another shot at the knothole and cackled loudly. "I just hit the target. Dead center. Guess I'll have to move back three feet. Getting too easy from here."

"I said we were crazy," Mack repeated. "A smart man would have taken that offer."

"Sure we're crazy, son. It'd be a mighty easy world for fellers like Lou Kyle if it wasn't for crazy jiggers like us."

Mack walked to the front door and stood, staring into the street. Evening shadows were beginning to fall across it as the day's warmth was blown away by a cold north wind riffling down from the Sundowns. Mack rolled a smoke, wondering what there was in some men that made them stubborn while others were as easily bent as a wheat straw in a gale. Two thousand dollars was more money than he'd ever seen. There were no tangible ties here in Axehandle to hold him. His store was a failure. Rosella would marry Kyle.

Yet now as he gave it thought, he knew there were friendship bonds holding him here, bonds that were far stronger to him than any money could forge. Jimmy Hinton, out in the desert, would need help. Soogan Wade would keep pressing him until Jimmy would have to go. There could be but one end to it. Inky Blair would eventually come to the place where he'd take a stand against Kyle, and he'd need help. Dad Perrod was too old to do the kind of day's work Kyle would demand of him. And Betty Grant! Mack smiled a little when he thought of her, for the thought was a pleasant one. Of all his friends she was the only one who would be able to stand on her own two feet.

It was then Mack saw the cavalcade turn into Main Street from the high desert road. A buckboard was in front, Soogan Wade driving, Rosella sitting beside him. Flanking the buckboard were two buckaroos, behind it the full string of Tomahawk riders. Mack ran his eyes back along the line and saw in surprise that Metolius Neele was not among them.

A hard-bitten, salty crew, these Tomahawk riders. None of them except Metolius Neele was his enemy, but on the other hand none was his friend. Somehow he had never quite fitted into the group. They respected him as a fighting man from the day he'd knocked Metolius Neele cold and wrecked the bunkhouse in the process. They'd let him alone after that, but they hadn't liked him. To most of them and particularly to George Queen, the ramrod, he was a nester lover, and for that reason he received indirectly some of the dislike they held for Jimmy Hinton.

The buckboard wheeled past the feed store, Soogan looking straight ahead and being careful not to see him. Rosella nodded and smiled, and Mack took a wicked enjoyment in hoping that Lou Kyle was watching. Some of the buckaroos pinned stony eyes upon him. Most of them followed George Queen's example and kept their gaze on the street ahead of them in the arrogant fashion befitting men who rode for the biggest outfit in the country.

Mack turned back into the store. He said gloomily: "Dad, I've got to get Jimmy off that homestead. Soogan ain't gonna fool with him much longer."

"You're wasting your wind and your time, son. Hell, Mack, he's happy. Let him alone. He'll stay there till he dies."

"Trouble is, dying may come purty quick for him."

"Jimmy never bothered nobody. He'll be all right." Dad rose from the sack of wheat where he had been sitting and stretched. "Reckon I'd better go get supper ready."

Mack sat down on the sack of wheat and rolled another smoke. Suddenly he came to a decision. He called: "Dad, just watch things. I'm going out."

He left the store and made the turn toward the hotel. It was Soogan Wade's habit to go there first with Rosella. Then

41

he'd drift into the Casino where he'd have a few drinks with his men. There would be no talking to him after he'd had those drinks.

Mack swung into the hotel lobby, saw that it was empty, and asked the clerk: "Soogan go out yet?"

"He's upstairs."

"Thanks."

Mack took a seat in the corner and threw his cigarette violently into a spittoon. There was no satisfaction in it. There was no satisfaction in anything unless it might be in pounding some sense into Soogan's head, a miracle Mack had little hope of accomplishing.

Mack saw Soogan come down the stairs, moving slowly as one who is tired and puzzled and feels suddenly the weight of time. He was a medium tall man whose wrinkled face was burned to a saddle-leather brown, and there was a mildly comical look about him that came from the huge, untrimmed mustache, a look that was totally deceptive, for Soogan Wade was anything but comical. His eyes were the real index of his character. They were bright and sharp, reflecting the aggressiveness that was so much a part of him.

Soogan Wade was not an old man as judged by the measure of time, but he had done three men's work back in the lean years when his outfit was one of a dozen small spreads on the high desert, and the hardships of those years had sapped much of the great, natural vitality from him. Now that the high desert was all Tomahawk range, Wade wanted everyone to know the distance he had come. It was that desire to flaunt his wealth that prompted him to substitute gold coins for buttons on his coat.

Mack rose and, stepping in front of Soogan before the cowman could reach the door, said: "Funny, what a man thinks he can do when he's riding plumb high and handsome."

"Get out of my way," Wade said darkly. "I haven't got time to swap gab with you."

"You can shove your tally book back into your desk," Mack went on as if he hadn't heard, "and it'll stay there, but damn it, Soogan, you can't treat people that way, and you're an old fool for thinking you can."

"And you're a young fool to think you could make the money Rosella's husband has got to have," Wade rasped. "I said to git out of my way. I'm looking for Natty Gordon."

"You're gonna listen if I have to rope and tie you, Soogan. Kyle says Rosella's gonna marry him. We'll leave me out of it. I ain't crying about myself because, if Rosella wanted to marry me bad enough, she wouldn't have let you bulldoze her into taking Kyle. I *am* hollering about what you're doing to her. If you had half the sense about men you've got about cows, you'd know damned well that Kyle wouldn't make a fitting husband for anybody you loved."

"You're jealous," Wade said truculently. "I ain't gonna bust 'em up just because you're sore you didn't get her."

"Soogan, there're only two things in life that mean a damn to you, Rosella and money. You figger, if you got 'em together, you'll have everything fixed. If you had the sense of a boiled sage hen, you'd know better."

Wade's face reddened under the pressure of his rising anger. "You ain't nothing but a buckaroo who thinks he's a businessman. You're going broke as fast as you can. Don't try telling me. . . ."

"All right." Mack gestured wearily. "I'm a buckaroo. I ain't a businessman. I oughta be out forking my sorrel and listening to a bunch of cows bawl. That ain't important one way or the other. I happen to love Rosella, and I want to see her happy."

"I've fixed Rosella's happiness. She's marrying the richest man in Axehandle. He'll be richer, too. Lou don't miss a bet."

"He don't for a fact," Mack agreed sourly. "He'd steal the gold fillings right out of your teeth when you yawned if you didn't watch him."

"You're worth thirty a month and beans and nothing more, Mack. Now you claim Lou Kyle is an ornery coyote who ain't fitting for Rosella to marry. Why? If you can't give me some damned good reasons, I'll figger you're just bellyaching because you lost your girl."

Mack could not make an answer that would satisfy Soogan Wade. He could put his fingers on no actual criminal act that Lou Kyle had done. His feeling about the man came from an accumulation of little things. He had known Kyle to close out dry farmers and small ranchers simply because he had the opportunity through the bank. Not once had he ever heard of Kyle's contributing a cent to any cause that didn't make him a profit. He interpreted every situation he met in terms of how it would affect him.

It was this ever-scheming selfishness about Kyle that told Mack he was not the man to give Rosella happiness, yet it would not be a sound argument to Soogan Wade, so he only said: "A man can't buy a woman's love, Soogan."

Wade snorted contemptuously. "Money will go a hell of a long ways toward it, son. I don't hold to this mush and tush about love nohow. Lou will build her the finest house in town. She'll have all the dresses she wants with lacy doodads on 'em, and she'll mix with the top crust of the country. She'll go to Portland, 'Frisco, Chicago. Hell, she'll go to Europe, if she wants to. You can't buy her that kind of foofaraw, and you never will."

"A woman wants something besides foofaraw. She. . . ."

"You ain't no expert on females," Wade said sharply, "and don't go to putting ideas into her head. Now I'm gonna find Natty Gordon."

Mack stepped away then and let Wade go by. Nothing could change the old man's mind about Lou Kyle. The bitter sourness of failure was in Mack as he stepped into the street. He had done all he could. What lay ahead for Rosella Wade would be of her own choosing.

"Mack," Inky Blair called. He came in a slow, lumbering run from the feed store. When he was closer, he panted: "I've been looking for you. Old Soogan's lost a lot of beef, Mack. The Tomahawk boys are down in the Casino talking about it. They're claiming Jimmy stole the critters, and they're fixing to swing him from a juniper limb."

Chapter Five

Natty Gordon centered the line of men along the bar in the Casino, Soogan Wade on one side of him, George Queen on the other. The deputy was a small, carefully dressed man who posed as the law in Axehandle. He held his job because he made it a cardinal principle never to cross important men like Lou Kyle and Soogan Wade. Now Gordon was pulling at his mustache, looking from Queen to Wade and back to Queen. He was worried, and he was scared, and Mack felt a contemptuous pity for him as he came up to the bar.

"I don't know what to do," Gordon was saying, his voice high and close to cracking from the tension under which he was laboring. "I don't know where to begin. You've had men on the range all winter, Soogan. If these cattle are gone, and there's no trace, I don't see what I can do."

"You can ride," Wade said belligerently. "Three hundred head of beef don't dig a hole and jump into it. Likewise they don't fly off. Now you find 'em, or I'll have your star."

"You wouldn't do that, Soogan," George Queen taunted. "He'd have to go to work if you did."

Gordon licked his lips nervously, saw Mack and Inky Blair, and asked: "You know that country, Mack. What do you think happened?"

"I haven't got the story." Mack hooked his thumbs in his belt and watched Soogan closely. "Don't look to me like it's anything to get worried about. I reckon Soogan could lose three hundred head without getting hurt much."

"We ain't gonna lose anything," Queen said darkly. He was a rail of a man, all bone and hide, the fat burned out of him in the long hours under a hot sun that had been his lot since

46

he was a boy. His eyes were hard and black, his mouth a thin slash across his face. He was tough, and he was proud, and his pride had been hurt. In the years he had rodded Tomahawk, there had been no great loss of cattle. There was a big loss now, and Queen was the kind who would hang a man for it. He might be wrong, but hang a man he would.

"It ain't a question of what I can afford," Wade said coldly. "That talk won't get us anything. The point is we've lost three hundred head. Mebbe more. They just disappeared into thin air. If we can lose three hundred head without leaving no trace, we can lose three thousand, and we can be cleaned."

"We ain't gonna lose anything," Queen repeated, black eyes pinned on Mack. "There's an answer, and it's so damned plain you're all overlooking it. Jimmy Hinton's squatting on our range, and he's a good friend of yours. Between you, you've got away with them cows, and I'm aiming to find out how you done it."

There was stunned silence for a moment. Natty Gordon's mouth came open in quick surprise. Wade's wrinkled face showed his amazement. Mack smiled thinly, his eyes locked with Queen's. He should have expected this. Metolius Neele had said almost the same thing the night before. Jimmy Hinton was the handiest man to blame, and Queen had to blame someone. Yet it seemed a little too pat.

"I've been called a lot of things," Mack said softly. A hand had come up to touch the crescent-shaped scar on his cheek. "Some things a man has to take, and some he don't. Being called a cow thief is one I don't take." His hand came down. "Start smoking your iron, George, or back up from that talk you just put out."

"No trouble, boys," Natty Gordon squealed.

"I don't back up for nobody," Queen said. "If you. . . ."

"Get down off your high horse, George," Wade bellowed.

"You ain't swapping no lead with Mack. Get your hand away from your iron. You hear me, George? If you're deaf, you ain't the man to rod Tomahawk."

Queen wasn't deaf. He straightened up, hand falling away from his gun. He shot a glance at Wade and then said hoarsely: "All right, Mack. Let's forget it."

Mack nodded. "That's fair enough, George." He looked at Wade. "Soogan, losing three hundred head on Tomahawk range is the craziest thing I ever heard of. It can't be done. You sure must've missed 'em sitting behind a juniper some-where."

"We didn't miss 'em," Wade said flatly. "We made a clean ride, and I tell you they're gone."

"You know the country better'n I do, but where would an outfit take three hundred head? North mebbe?"

"No, I reckon not." Wade frowned. "There ain't no water in them Sundowns. It's too long a drive to get 'em to water, and the country's too rough. Likewise they couldn't go east for the same reason."

"Mebbe they went west," Gordon jeered. "Flew across Pioneer Cañon."

Wade shook his head. "That's for you to find out. I don't know. They didn't come south, or they'd have been seen. Too many people living down there."

"I ain't eating what I'm gonna say now," Queen grated. "I say Hinton is the one. There ain't nobody else. Any ornery critter who'd steal a spring and turn it into a hog waller would steal cows."

"You'd sure like to pin this on Jimmy, wouldn't you?" Mack asked contemptuously. "Use your noggin, George. You just heard Soogan say they couldn't go east, west, north, or south. That just about takes care of all the directions but up and down. Now, considering the country, what would Jimmy do with them cow critters?"

"He could feed 'em to his hogs."

"And hide 'em in the pig pens till the hogs ate 'em? George, you ain't even bright."

"He's right up there against the foothills of the Sundowns," the Tomahawk ramrod said doggedly. "Mebbe he found a spring back in them mountains. There's a mess of little cañons, criss-crossing back and forth. Might be he hid 'em somewhere. You could look till hell froze over before you'd ever find 'em."

"Soogan said you hadn't found any tracks," Mack objected.

"There's a lot of lava up there by Round Butte. Cows wouldn't leave no tracks in that stuff. What ain't lava is sand. Tracks could be brushed out right behind the cows."

"He couldn't take 'em on through. What would he do with 'em?"

"The railroad's coming in this year," Queen answered, "and railroad men eat a lot of meat. I dunno how he figures on getting the beef to 'em, but I've got a month's pay that says that's what he's up to."

"And you figger a man like Jimmy could handle that many cows by himself?" Mack demanded.

Queen shrugged. "Might be somebody's helping him."

Mack laid his gaze on Wade's face. "Soogan, you've never liked Jimmy because he's the only nester who ever squatted on Tomahawk range with enough guts to listen to your threats and get shot at and still stick."

"He's got guts," Wade admitted grudgingly, "but I'll get him out o' there. You can count on it."

"Would it be you're dreaming up this cow-stealing yarn just to give you an excuse to pour it into Jimmy?"

"Hell, no," Wade bellowed. "I ain't that ornery."

There was a ring of sincerity in the old man's voice that told Mack he'd made the wrong guess, but there was no mistaking what was in George Queen's mind. Mack said sharply: "Natty, there was some talk about that big juniper back of Jimmy's cabin bearing fruit. It wouldn't look good for your record if you had a hanging, would it?"

The scared look was back on the deputy's face. He shot a glance at Queen. "You wouldn't let your boys do that, would you, George?" he quavered.

Queen's grin was quick and wicked. "I can't say what my boys would do on a dark night, but I'm telling you one thing. Hinton would sure be smart to get off Tomahawk range."

"If you swing Jimmy, George," Mack said slowly and deliberately, "I'm coming after you, and Soogan won't keep your hide from getting some holes drilled through it." He turned back to Wade. "Soogan, why couldn't the Carne boys have done the job?"

"Because the gate ain't far from our watering place on the creek," Soogan said quickly, "and some of the boys would have seen 'em. Besides, the dirt's 'dobe there, and it'd sure hold tracks in the spring when it's wet. We never found any. No, it ain't the Carne boys, that's sure."

Mack nodded and, wheeling away, walked rapidly toward the feed store, with Inky Blair in a heavy-footed run, trying to keep up with him.

"You don't need to be in such a danged hurry," Inky complained. "Every time I try to keep up with you, I lose my breath, and it takes me a week to find it."

"Get some hounds and track it," Mack growled. "It's stout enough to track." He turned into the store and went on into the back room. "Supper ready, Dad?"

"No, it ain't," Perrod answered. "I didn't know when you'd be back."

"It's all right. I'll eat at Betty's. Go get a horse for me. Better let me have your roan. My sorrel's kind of tuckered."

"I'll get him," Perrod said and shuffled out.

Mack picked up his Winchester and cut across the street to the Top Notch. He leaned the rifle against the counter, swung a leg over a stool, and sat down. "Steak and onions, Betty," he said, "and make it quick. I've got riding to do."

Inky came in and sat down beside Mack. "Hod dang it, feller, you sure do keep on the move. Toss a steak on for me, Betty." He ran a sleeve across his fat face. "Looks like trouble's boiling up all around us, don't it?"

"It does for a fact," Mack answered, and fell again into silence.

Inky inspected the sugar bowl. He called: "Bring in the sugar, Betty. This bowl's almost empty. It isn't more'n half full." He looked sideways at Mack, but neither spoke until Betty came with the steaks. Then Inky pointed to Mack's Winchester. "He's going hunting again, Betty."

"What is it this time?" Betty asked.

"Coyotes," Mack answered.

That was all Mack said. He ate rapidly, as if time were rushing away from him and there was too little of it. These two who knew him well said nothing, but, when he was done, and Betty had filled his cup again with coffee, she said: "Let me go with you, Mack. I was raised with a Colt in my hand in the Piute country."

"Thanks, Betty, but I'd do less worrying about you if you were here."

"I'd go, too," Inky said, "if I could find a horse that would carry me. I can't hit nothing with a gun, but I could furnish some support."

"You could support a cannon," Mack said dryly. "Tell Dad to keep an eye on things." Mack picked up his rifle and stepped to the door. He glanced back at Betty, thinking of her offer, and thinking, too, it was something Rosella would not have done. Then he went out, mounted, and rode away.

It was dusk when Mack reached the rim above Axehandle. He rested the roan, staring down at the scattered lights that were coming to life in the little town. *Lou Kyle's town,* Mack was thinking. *Rosella was there, and probably she was with Kyle now, listening to him tell her about the foofaraw he'd be buying her.* Then Mack turned his horse eastward along the county road and put his mind to this new problem. Mack, knowing George Queen's character well, was certain that the danger threatening Jimmy Hinton was real and imminent.

Full darkness came before Mack reached the road that turned north to Carne Cove. The last of the day had gone, and in its place were stars and a full moon. It was a strange and awesome world by night, a vast and endless expanse of sage and bunchgrass and junipers. He rode steadily north, the land tilting upward as he came closer to the Sundowns. He passed the log gate barring the road into the cove, wondered idly if Cat Carne stood guard there by night as well as by day, and kept on. The smooth, cone shape of Round Butte appeared, and he was in the lava. There were patches of an old flow behind him such as the one at the Carne gate, but here the volcanic action had been recent.

"Round Butte blew its head off perhaps two centuries ago," Jimmy Hinton had once said. "Practically yesterday."

"Yesterday?" Mack had laughed. "How would you figger a week, Jimmy?"

"Geologically speaking, two centuries ago is a mere nothing. It's all a matter of relationship. A man is born and lives and dies in a span of time that is less than the tick of a watch, Mack. You can't define time any more than you can define God. There's no telling how long it took Him to shape the world we take in such a matter-of-fact way. Some of these old lava caves and flows were made five thousand years ago. Maybe ten thousand." Then his eyes had twinkled. "If you really want to talk about time, go back to the age of the reptiles. Or take the days when the rhinos, three-toed horses, and oreodonts roamed around what we call the John Day country. Why, there were sycamore forests growing millions of years ago even before the mammals came."

"I'll take a common old cottonwood or a juniper," Mack had said, "and any old rattler, sunning himself on top of Round Butte will do for a reptile as far as I'm concerned. I don't see no sense in worrying about them times. We've got enough trouble now."

But Jimmy had grinned and shaken his head. "You're a man of action, Mack, and there is no part of a scientist in you. What I'm trying to say is that we aren't very important, and our troubles aren't important. I mean in the long pull. We think they are because we're so close to them. We don't have any perspective. Perhaps these things that happened a long time ago may influence your life a great deal. For instance, what Round Butte blew out of its stomach two centuries ago might determine the day and year you die."

Mack was thinking about that conversation now as the roan made his way over a lava upthrust and came down to the flat, sand-topped earth beyond it. He didn't expect to change Jimmy Hinton's mind and persuade him to come to town any more than he had expected to change Soogan Wade's ideas about Rosella's marrying Kyle, but he had to make the try. Besides, he wanted to have a look at the dry Sundowns beyond Jimmy's cabin. It was an impossible hiding place for cattle, yet it was the only one.

In the back of his mind, Mack admitted grudgingly, was Wade's statement that he was a buckaroo worth his thirty a month and beans and nothing more. It would be worth a great deal to prove the old man wrong. It would be worth even more to prove to Soogan Wade that he was wrong about Lou Kyle. An idea came to Mack's mind then, an idea that shocked him. Perhaps it was Kyle's smart, scheming brain that was behind the cattle theft. Immediately Mack put the notion out of his mind. It was fantastic that a man in Kyle's position would steal three hundred head of beef.

Ahead of Mack a light in the window of Jimmy Hinton's cabin was shining like a small, earth-bound star. Mack was surprised to see it. It was in the early hours of the morning, and he had not expected to find Hinton still up. He rode directly toward the cabin, passing alongside another twisted pile of lava, looming ghost-like beside the trail. Reining up in the fringe of light, he called: "Hello the house."

Mack waited, drawing his gun and holding it ready for action, as he sat motionless in the saddle. The door was swung open, and a flood of lamplight washed out. Jimmy Hinton stood there, his lank body a high silhouette in the rectangular frame.

"You make a target as big as a house," Mack called sharply. "Jimmy, you danged, lame-brained fool, don't you know that's no way to come out of a house?"

"Sounds like my rough-talking friend named Mack Jarvis." Hinton came across the yard. "Step down and come in. I was about ready for breakfast."

Mack dismounted, still feeling the prod of gusty anger. "Look, Jimmy, I'll tell you something I've only told you ten times. You're squatting on Tomahawk range. George Queen and his boys are pretty salty *hombres*. One of these days they'll call to you like I did, you'll open the door and stand there like you was Queen of the May, and they'll gut shoot you."

"Gut shooting is a bad practice," Hinton said distastefully. "Causes a lot of leaks."

"You idiot," Mack groaned. "You crazy idiot. I don't know why I rode clear out here to hell and gone just to tell you you're in trouble. I sure won't change the way you do things."

"Now that you're done belittling my intelligence," Hinton said amiably, "let's put your animal away. Then I'll brew up a pot of coffee."

"Don't you ever sleep?" Mack asked as Hinton led the way toward the log barn.

"Oh, I sleep in the daytime and read most of the night. I like the night quiet for reading. There's something about the day noises that bothers me."

"I'll bet you get some real rackets around here in the daytime, all right," Mack jeered. "Mebbe you even hear your hogs grunt."

"It's annoying," Hinton admitted. "I have been thinking I'd drive them all to town."

"Then Tomahawk cattle could water at your spring. That's the most sensible thing I ever heard you say, Jimmy."

Hinton fumbled in his pocket for a match and lit a lantern hanging inside the door. He peered at Mack through his thick glasses as if not sure what had prompted his friend to say what he had. Then he nodded. "I guess they could, Mack. I don't need all the water for my lawn and garden."

"It insults Soogan to think that you turned your spring into a hog waller. Mebbe he'd let you stay if you got rid of them critters."

Hinton said nothing as he forked hay into a manger. Later, after he had put out the lantern and was shutting the barn door, the flat, echoing sound of a gunshot rode the night air to them — then another, and a third, and that was all. The silence of the high desert was around them again. There was the faint whisper of wind through the junipers. The screech of an owl and the faint cry of a coyote from some rim in the

55

Sundowns came to them.

For a full five minutes neither man moved. Then Hinton said: "I've never heard a gunshot at night during all the months I've lived here. There's nobody closer than the Carne brothers or possibly a Tomahawk rider. What do you think it means?"

"I don't know," Mack answered, "but it isn't good. There hasn't been any trouble on this range since Soogan got rid of his neighbors, but there's trouble shaping up now, and you're in the middle of it."

"That so?" Hinton asked carelessly. "Well, I guess we all need a little spice in our living."

It was not until Hinton had stoked up his fire and had the coffee on the stove that he settled down beside Mack.

"What's this trouble you've been working up to, Mack?"

"Soogan lost three hundred head of beef, and George Queen allows you're the monkey that got 'em."

Hinton laughed and reached for his pipe and tobacco can on the table. "Where does Queen think I'd put three hundred head of cattle if I were a good enough man to steal them?"

Hinton sat, puffing on his pipe, while Mack told him what had happened. He was an older man than Mack with thin, sandy hair, round shoulders, and a pair of gray eyes that were bloodshot from hours of night reading. He was a strange man to find on a lonely homestead in this primitive land, but somehow he had made the transition from city life speedily and with little discomfort. Jimmy Hinton knew a great deal about a great many things, but his knowledge brought him no happiness. Somewhere along his back trail he had received a soul-twisting experience that had driven him from human association into this lonely existence where he had only a horse, his pigs, and the raw elements of nature for company. Mack could not guess what that experience had been, but he did know that it had made a recluse out of Hinton.

56

When Mack had finished talking, Hinton got up, poured the coffee, and handed Mack a cup. He sat down again, knocked out his pipe, and slowly refilled it. "That's interesting and crazy, Mack. I don't believe Soogan lost any beef. I think he's trying to work up a situation whereby he will have an excuse to kill me."

"I accused him of that, but he denied it. It looked to me like he was telling the truth, Jimmy. I know Soogan pretty well. He's tough and ornery, but he's got some good points, and telling the truth is one of 'em."

Hinton shrugged. "Thanks for riding out, friend. It's proof that there are still a few decent people in the world. Not many, mind you, but a few. What do you say about going to bed?"

"How about coming to town, Jimmy, and staying with me and Dad Perrod till this blows over?"

"Dad Perrod is again one of these decent people who is living proof that a few of the breed still survive, but I'd rather stay here. Let them come."

"You're so damned smart, you're a fool," Mack groaned. "If you live to be a hundred, you'll never savvy gents like George Queen and Metolius Neele. They'll hang you higher'n hell, Jimmy, whether you ever stole a cow or not, and Natty Gordon wouldn't touch 'em."

"What difference would it make if they did hang me? The pain would not last long. I would soon be dead, and my troubles would be over. Let's talk about something pleasant like you and the beautiful Rosella."

Mack got up and walked to the stove. He refilled his cup with coffee and stood in silence for a moment, staring at the black liquid. He said dully: "That isn't pleasant, either, Jimmy. She's marrying Lou Kyle."

"She . . . why, I thought she was waiting for you to make your first million so you could qualify with old Soogan."

"So did I, but I guess I wasn't making that million fast enough."

Hinton got up and came to Mack. He said softly: "A woman did that to me, Mack. She was beautiful like Rosella, and a beautiful woman will attract bad men as well as the good. Since then I've been waiting for death to release my errant soul from its bodily prison. That's why I'm what you call a fool. Each day is a day of soul-searching torture. I have no ambition left in me. There's nothing I want to accomplish before I die. Mack, don't let her do that to you."

A one-sided grin came to Mack's lips. "I don't aim to let that happen. There's a thing or two I'm going to do before I cash in. I'd like to see the Pioneer Valley people get a square deal on a few things, and, to do that, I'm going to have to whittle Lou Kyle down a notch or two."

"A worthy ambition," Hinton said heavily. "Let's go to bed."

When Mack was in his bunk, and the lamp had been blown out, a swarm of thoughts swept through his mind, the dark thoughts of a man who faces a task he knows he cannot do. If this were a job that he could put his hands on, a horse to be ridden or a house to be built or a man to fight, he'd know what to do. But this was different. He had no weapon to combat human indifference. Hinton would stay here, and he'd die. Mack was a spectator, watching fate twist a hideous, cruel pattern, and finding himself without power to influence the shaping of that pattern.

The throb of talk woke Mack from a deep well of sleep. Hinton's bunk was empty. Mack saw that, he heard the snap of burning wood in the stove, and he wished dully that whoever was talking would go away. He wasn't done sleeping. Weariness from the long night ride was still in him. Hinton would sleep all day, but he couldn't. He had more riding to do in the Sundowns.

The thought came to Mack's sleep-fogged brain that Hinton was talking to his hogs. Hinton should know better. He knew Mack wanted to sleep. Of all the damned fool things for a man to do! Get up at daybreak to talk to a bunch of hogs. Then it occurred to Mack that he didn't have quite the right explanation for the conversation. One of the voices wasn't Hinton's, and it wasn't a hog talking back.

Then another voice, loud and cruel, swept the last cobwebs of sleep from Mack's brain. It said: "Throw out a loop, Metolius. We're gonna stop this cow stealing, and do it permanent. That limb on the north side of the juniper will hold him all right." It was George Queen's voice. Mack had heard it too often to be mistaken.

Mack leaped from the bunk and ran to the window. Hinton stood halfway between the barn and the cabin, his hands in the air, his long-jawed face without expression. A half dozen Tomahawk riders sat in their saddles in front of him, naked guns in their hands. Back of Queen was a horse with the still form of a buckaroo tied face down across the saddle.

Metolius Neele was building a loop, a cruel, satisfied grin on his lips. He said: "All set, George. Let's get it over with."

Chapter Six

Mack, clad only in his drawers, grabbed up his Winchester from the corner where he'd dropped it the night before and jerked the door open. He called: "George, I shoot pretty well with this blow pipe. Want to see?"

George Queen wouldn't have looked more surprised if Round Butte had spewed a hot rock out of its crater and dropped it on the ground in front of him. He laughed, but there was little humor in the high cackle that came from him. He said: "You sure look funny in them drawers, Mack. You oughta go put your pants on."

"I don't reckon I look any funnier than you did, George, when you first saw me. You figgered it'd be plumb easy, riding in on a feller who ain't really what you'd call a fighting man, getting the drop on him, and stringing him up. Yes sir, you boys were sure taking chances. You're a bunch of ring-tailed wowsers, now, ain't you?"

Mack's tone had the slashing force of a blacksnake, cutting Queen across the face. Every Tomahawk man from Queen on around to Metolius Neele looked ashamed. None of them spoke, nor did any of them make the slightest move, for there was a quality about Mack's face that told them the first one to make a move would die.

Suddenly Hinton laughed. It was a soft, contemptuous sound. He moved toward Mack as he said: "You must have put salt on their tails, Mack. I never saw six mean, murder-talking men get tamed in so short a time."

Mack didn't take his eyes from George Queen. Metolius Neele was the toughest man in the bunch, but it was Queen's job to make the decision to fight and die, or live to fight again.

Mack said: "I figger I've got hold of the jerkline, gents. If any of you think different, start smoking."

Still they didn't move, and they didn't speak. Five of them were watching Queen, and Queen was watching Mack. The ramrod couldn't make up his mind. He'd backed water the afternoon before in the Casino, and it wasn't in him to do it again. The silence ran on, stretching every man's nerves to the breaking point. It could not go on much longer. Mack, sensing it, and knowing no real gain could come from such a fight, said: "Drop your irons, gents. I'm not gonna stand here and augur all morning. The air's a mite chilly for a feller in my shape."

They let their Colts go then, relief showing in their faces as they relaxed from the tension that had gripped them. Queen jerked a thumb at the dead man. "It's Curly Isher, Mack. We found him the other side of Round Butte."

"Why were you after Jimmy?" Mack asked.

Queen pulled a thin book from his coat pocket. "This has got Hinton's name on it. We found it about ten feet from Curly's body. He was plugged three times. Looked to me like somebody had been talking to him. The killing son-of-a-bitch was up close when he let Curly have it."

"Any sign?"

"Nothing but this book." Queen glanced at the name. "*Macbeth*, it says. I don't know who this Macbeth *hombre* was, but I figger he didn't walk over there and lay down by himself. Knowing the way Natty Gordon enforces the law, we figgered we'd square up for Curly ourselves."

"Jimmy didn't do it, George. In the first place, he can't shoot a gun worth a damn. Not even up close. I've seen him try. In the second place, Curly wouldn't let Jimmy get close to him because both you and Metolius said you figgered he'd been doing the stealing, so I reckon Curly would have been suspicious of him, too. In the third place, Jimmy wouldn't be reading that book in the moonlight while he waited for Curly to come up."

Queen cuffed back his Stetson and scratched his head. "I reckon part of that's sense all right," he admitted reluctantly. "Soogan sent Curly and Metolius up here to the north range to keep an eye on things, and Metolius told Curly to stay clear of Hinton. We figgered he'd give himself away if we watched him for a week or so."

"That right, Metolius?"

Neele swore under his breath. He shook his head, ran the back of a hand over his flat nose, and growled: "That's right, damn it. Curly would have recognized Hinton in the moonlight."

"Were you anywhere around the butte last night?"

"I was over at the lava field," Neele said.

"Then you heard the shooting?"

"Yeah, I heard it, but, when I got there, Curly was dead, and I couldn't find nothing but this book."

Mack swung back to face Queen. He asked: "George, how did you and the rest of your bunch get here so quick?"

"Soogan sent us out. He got to thinking Metolius and Curly wasn't enough. I'd told Metolius I'd send somebody from town this morning and for him to wait at Round Butte. He was sitting there when we rode up. Now what do you know about this, Mack?"

"I know Jimmy didn't do it. I got here about two, three o'clock. We'd just put my horse away when we heard the shooting."

Metolius looked at Queen meaningly. The ramrod nodded. "I reckon you're lying, Mack, to cover up. How'd your book get out there, nester, if you didn't lose it?"

"I had some things stolen several days ago," Hinton said.

"I don't know who did it. It was early in the morning. Just about this time. I was going into the pig pen when somebody hit me on the head and knocked me cold. There were several things taken from the cabin."

"Like what?" Queen asked.

"My knife, a pipe that I've smoked for years, and that copy of *Macbeth* you found."

Queen shifted in his saddle. "That yarn is just loco enough to be true. Whoever done the killing might have wanted to pin it on Hinton. They'd know we'd jump him just like we done."

"Mebbe somebody wants Jimmy off this range besides Tomahawk," Mack suggested.

"Yeah," Queen agreed somberly. "You gonna let us ride now?"

"Have I got your word you won't be back after Jimmy?"

"Not unless we hit onto something more'n we've got now. We're taking Curly into town and telling Gordon about it. That dude won't do nothing, but we'll tell him."

"All right." Mack lowered his Winchester. "Pick up your hardware and vamoose."

Metolius Neele stepped down, handed the six-guns and rifles to the mounted men, and holstered his own Colt. Then, with his Winchester in his hand, he wheeled to face Mack, his eyes bright and wicked. "I ain't never forgot what you done to me, Jarvis. I'd have settled with you when you was riding for Tomahawk, but Soogan wouldn't let me. I'd have got you the other night when I caught you with Rosella if she hadn't got the bulge on me. Next time" — he jabbed a bony finger at Mack — "there won't be any ifs. There's them that figgers your carcass is worth one thousand dollars. It'll make me real happy to collect that *dinero*."

"Any time," Mack murmured.

Mack watched Neele closely, but the man made no hostile move. He swung into saddle, reined in behind Queen, and the six of them rode away, the last rider leading the dead man's horse.

"I guess I'm not as ready to die as I thought I was." Hinton ran a shaking hand over his face. "If you hadn't taken part in the trouble, I'd have had my neck stretched."

"They were fixing to do it," Mack agreed. "I knew the way Queen was talking last night that he'd try it. Then they ran onto Curly, and that gave 'em all the excuse they needed. Now I'm gonna put my pants on before I freeze complete."

Hinton filled the stove with wood and then stood with his back to it. "They don't really think I stole that bunch of cattle, do they, Mack?"

"I don't think they do," Mack answered. "It's partly a proposition of getting you out of the way, but it's mostly that Queen will feel better if he can string somebody up. Mebbe there won't be any more stealing, and he can tell Soogan he's fixed everything."

"I'll have to finish feeding the pigs. You start the coffee, Mack."

The coffee was boiling, and Mack was slicing bacon, when Hinton returned.

"Hell of a way to treat a visitor," Mack said in an aggrieved tone. "Making him get breakfast."

"It is," Hinton agreed. "Sit down. I'll finish the meal." He began stirring up a batch of biscuits. "Mack, it's probably presumptuous for me to offer any explanations for the way these cows have disappeared, you knowing the country and the people as you do, but I've been thinking it over, and I'd like to see it stopped. I'll fight for my rights as homesteader, but being accused of cattle stealing is more than I can stand. I've never been called a thief before."

64

"You ain't as thick-skinned as you were last night," Mack observed.

"No, I'm not. I had too close a look at that rope in Neele's hands. Did you ever come that close to being hanged?"

"Never did."

"When we analyze this situation, we can discount the supernatural." Hinton slid a pan of biscuits into the oven. "We can discount me as a suspect. That leaves two possibilities. Perhaps Queen and Neele and some more or all of Soogan's men stole the cattle themselves."

"I don't think so." Mack shook his head. "Don't forget I've worked with most of those *hombres*, Jimmy. They're salty as they come, but it don't strike me they're thieves. Metolius mebbe, but not Queen."

"All right." Hinton gestured as if to wave that suggestion away. "Number two. I thought of this last night when you were telling me what took place in the Casino. Soogan admitted that the cattle could not have been driven out of the country in any direction. You said that left up and down. Cows wouldn't go up, but they could go down. It's my idea that the Carne brothers have stolen the cattle and have hidden them in the cove."

"I asked Soogan about it last night. He figgered some of his boys would have seen 'em chousing the cows through the gate."

"There might be another way known only to the Carnes," Hinton insisted.

"Now look," Mack said patiently, "the east side of the cove is a drop straight down, and, besides, the northern part of the rim has got a lava flow along it that makes a wall ten feet high or better. But supposing the Carnes did get the cows down there. Where would they keep 'em so you couldn't see 'em from the rim?"

65

"I don't know." Hinton took the biscuits out of the oven. "Everything has a logical explanation. Why don't you ask Soogan Wade and Gordon to go to the bottom of the cove with you?"

"We'd get our ears shot off." Mack pulled a chair back and sat down at the table. "I like my ears, son."

When they had finished eating, Hinton drew his pipe and tobacco from his pocket, and leaned back in his chair. "Mack, I've never bothered anybody here. I thought I was getting as far away from civilization as I could. Still, I find myself pulled into the vortex of a fight that is utterly petty and of no moment to anybody."

"Losing three hundred head of cows ain't exactly petty," Mack said dryly.

"It isn't enough to hang a man for," Hinton insisted.

"George Queen thinks so." Mack rose and reached for his Stetson. "Funny thing about the Tomahawk boys. There ain't a better bunch of buckaroos in Oregon. They'd take a herd to hell, and, if there wasn't no market there, they'd fetch them back and sell 'em somewhere else."

"Then, when something doesn't suit them, they become killers. I don't know, Mack. Goodness and badness is a matter of relativity."

Mack stood by the door, a frown furrowing his forehead. "You're a little over my head, Jimmy. You think too much, which is a trouble I don't have. I know what I'm going to do."

"Let's give it a test, Mack." Hinton smiled. "What will you do if Rosella sees her mistake in time and decides she'd rather marry you than Kyle?"

"Why, I'd marry her today if she said so," Mack said quickly. "I'm not a complete damn' fool."

"You'd be a damn' fool if you married her after she broke her promise to you. Mack, I thought once I knew what love

66

was, but I doubt now that I ever did. Do you think you ever really loved Rosella?"

"Think?" Mack exploded. "Hell, I know. When Kyle made that announcement in the Casino, I felt like a mule had kicked me in the belly. Sure I love her."

Hinton laid a match flame to his pipe. He watched Mack through the smoke, as if turning something over in his mind that he wasn't sure should be said. Then he blew out the match, his decision made. "Mack, you were an orphan. All your life you've envied people who had homes and families and the security of a settled life. Isn't your loving Rosella a case of finding a girl who was pretty and desirable, and fitting her into the dreams you'd held all through the years?"

"No," Mack said roughly. "She's mine. She belongs to me. She loves me. It's just that Soogan has preached money to her all her life, and. . . ." He saw that Hinton did not believe him, and suddenly he saw the weakness in what he was saying. Whatever preaching about money Soogan had done, whatever pressure he had put upon her, the fact remained that the choice had been hers.

"I'm not the one who should give advice," Hinton said heavily, "but it's what I'm going to do. I was hurt, so I've crawled away to die. You're different, Mack. You've got drive and vitality for a dozen men. That's why I don't want Rosella to do to you what was done to me. Get out of the country. Forget her. She's fickle, and she'd give you nothing but heartaches all your life, if you did marry her. You'd only have half her heart. She's chosen money. . . ."

Black fury was in Mack Jarvis then. He took a step toward Hinton, a great fist balled, a fierce desire in him to smash back into Jimmy Hinton the words he'd spoken. Hinton did not back away. He stood beside the table, eyes blinking at Mack through the thick glasses, fear not a part of him.

Mack's fist fell to his side. He wheeled out of the cabin and strode to the log barn. Hinton followed him and stood, watching in silence while Mack saddled the roan. Then he said somberly: "If I have offended you, Mack, I can only offer my apologies. There was a moment when I was alive again. It seemed to me I was living through you and being able to do the things I should have done and never had the courage to do. For a moment I forgot I owed my life to you. I offer my thanks, and my apologies."

"You owe me neither." A small smile touched Mack's lips, the fury dead in him. "I'm going into the Sundowns just to satisfy myself that Soogan's cows weren't driven back there and held by some outside outfit. I'll be back in a few days. Mebbe a week."

"You will find it dry traveling," Hinton warned. "I've been all over those mountains, and I've found two little springs. One's just above the rim five miles from here. The other one's on the north side of Bull Mountain. Neither one is big enough to water a dozen cows."

"I'll find 'em. Thanks, Jimmy."

Hinton nodded as Mack turned his roan toward the mountains.

Mack rode until evening, going deeper into the Sundowns than he ever had before. It was a wild and useless country of deep cañons, rimrock, and thickets of jackpine. More than once he turned a bend in the cañon he was following and found himself directly in front of a cliff three hundred feet high. Then he was forced to backtrack and spend an hour searching for a way through. It would be impossible, he thought, for any cattle thieves, no matter how skillful, to drive a herd through such country.

Once he came to Pioneer Cañon, he let his horse stand for

a time on the rim. Directly below him was the sparkling turbulence of the creek, three hundred feet from where he sat his saddle. It might well have been fifty times that, for all the value the water was to cattle grazing in the mountains. Across the cañon the Sundowns were far less rugged than this spur on the east side of the creek. On the other side of the cañon there was water, a good stand of merchantable timber, and large meadows of lush grass. A dozen small cattle outfits were scattered from Axehandle to the summit. It was the untapped riches of that section which had lured the railroad up to Pioneer Creek.

Mack turned his roan north, followed a spine-like ridge, and came down into a cross-cañon. Here he made a small fire, cooked his dinner, and went on. Near evening he killed a buck, dressed it, and found the spring Jimmy Hinton had said was on Bull Mountain. There he made camp. He sat by the fire for a time after supper, thinking of what Hinton had said about Rosella, and feeling a sour shame for the anger Hinton's words had raised in him.

Twilight came, and night, and the stars made a bright shining over him. He was almost asleep when he heard stealthy steps moving through the jackpines. He slid away from the low-burning fire, pausing in the black shadow of a high boulder. Drawing his gun, he hunkered there, motionless. For a time there was no sound.

The moon rose, throwing the jackpines into sharp relief. Mack thought first of Metolius Neele who might have followed him, of Cat Carne, and then of Lou Kyle, but now, as he remained motionless in the shadows, he could think of no reason for Kyle paying that kind of money for his death.

Mack heard the steps then and tensed, finger tight against the trigger. Instantly the tension left him, for the man had come into the firelight. It was Natty Gordon.

"I oughta drill you," Mack said sharply, "just for coming up on me that way. You're a hell of a lawman, Natty."

"I won't augur." Gordon held out his hands to the fire. "What are you doing here?"

"Trying to find them cows George Queen said Jimmy had back here." Mack threw wood on the fire and looked at the deputy in the light of the quick blaze. Dust and weariness laid a shadow over Gordon. He was far from the perfectly clad figure he always was in town. He built a smoke, shoulders hunched forward, an unhappy little man who held no hope of finding what he had set out to find.

"I'm here on the same wild goose chase." Gordon picked up a burning limb, lighted his cigarette, and tossed the limb back into the fire. "It's a damned mean, dry country. I'll bet my bottom dollar there ain't a cow on this side of Hinton's homestead."

"I don't think so, either, but I'm going to explore this country just on the off chance there might be a hole in the ground where three hundred head could be held. Then I'm going back, and I'm going to stuff George's lie down his throat. Somebody's covering somebody else, Natty, and it ain't Jimmy."

"Mebbeso," Gordon said dully. "Mind if I camp here tonight?"

"Go get your horse. I suppose you thought you'd found the cow thieves when you saw my fire."

"I was scared I had," Natty admitted. He got up. "You shouldn't be too sure about Hinton, Mack. Might be some other place where he's got 'em. I'm gonna keep my eyes on him."

"He'll sure be worried. Mebbe them cows did grow wings, Natty, and flew across Pioneer Cañon. That's what you'd better look for. An old pile of cow wings. You know how white faces

70

arc. They always lose their wings in the spring."

"I'll watch for 'em," Gordon said dryly and walked away.

Natty Gordon left the next morning, growling that there wasn't any sense in him getting saddle blisters traipsing over the country when the whole Tomahawk crew couldn't find three hundred cows.

Mack stayed in the Sundowns for a week, riding north to the summit and beyond, and east to where the jackpine-clad mountains gave way to a broken sage-covered country. Not once did he find the slightest indication that cattle had ever been held in this spur of the Sundowns, or had been driven through to the wheat country beyond. Then, satisfied that Soogan Wade's cattle had not gone out this way, he broke camp and rode back to Hinton's cabin, coming in at dusk.

"I'm glad you're back," Hinton said worriedly. "I've never seen a country where the wildness seemed to flow out of the cañon like it does up here."

"It's wild all right, and it never saw a cow." Mack waved a big hand in a gesture of futility. "I wish George Queen had taken that ride with me."

They talked that evening of everything except Lou Kyle and Rosella, but mostly about the cattle theft, going over it time after time, and finding nothing new. Hinton got up and paced the floor, pulling steadily at his pipe. "I tell you it's got to be the Carnes. I don't know how they did it, but they got those cows down the cañon wall and hid them. I always arrive at that conclusion by the process of elimination."

"You're sure hipped on the idea," Mack grumbled.

"I'm going to do some spying," Hinton said savagely. "Next time you ride this way, I'll have evidence." He picked up a large gray stone, standing in the corner, and tossed it to Mack. "What do you think of that?"

"Pumice." Mack lifted it and laid it down. "Weighs about as much as a bushel of feathers. Lots of it in this country."

"I picked this piece up on the other side of Round Butte. The stuff always fascinates me. It's actually foam on a lava floor, you know. Formed when Round Butte blew up, I suppose. Sort of a volcanic glass."

"What did you bring it home for?"

"It's fine for cleaning out a burned pan." Hinton smiled. "The old-timers used it on their bunions. It's a great country here, Mack. Funny how I never thought about it until I saw that rope in Neele's hand the other day. I'm going to start living again."

"Then you'll come . . . ?"

"No, I'm not leaving here," Hinton said quickly. "I'm going to stay. You can call me a fool again, but I'm staying. I've been a coward all my life. I'm not running any more."

Mack, seeing the new strength that was in his friend's face, said: "All right, Jimmy. Play your hand out the way you want to." He picked up the pumice. "Talk about this being a strange country, they say rock floats and wood sinks. There's petrified wood on the other side of Pioneer Creek."

"I've seen some of it."

"Another yarn they tell is about a couple of dudes who were fishing in one of the lakes down below here a piece. They didn't have an anchor, so they picked up a big hunk of this, put it in the boat, and, when they got out a ways, they tied their rope onto the pumice and threw it out. It wasn't much of an anchor. Bobbed along like a chunk of cork."

Hinton didn't laugh. He had opened the door and stood there, his eyes on the cone-like blot Round Butte made against the sky. Suddenly he turned, shut the door, and came close to where Mack sat. He said, his voice charged with emotion: "Mack, I've done a lot of talking I thought I meant, and now

72

know I didn't. I want to live to do some of the things I should have been doing when I was sitting out here in a wilderness, reading Shakespeare, and telling myself what a terrible world it was. The only reason it is a terrible world is because idiots like me don't do something about the scoundrels who pull everything in for themselves. I had never thought about it that way until I saw you, standing there with a rifle in your hands, making six good men out of six tough ones in less time than I could whistle."

"Now hold onto your lines a minute . . . ," Mack began.

"Just one more thing," Hinton cut in. "This fight you're into with Kyle ain't just for you or Rosella. It's for everybody who lives in this country. All the people who have been squeezed and hurt and perhaps killed because of Kyle's greed. Anyhow, I want to help fight him. This cabin is built over a cave, one of those little lava caves like you find all over the country. In case I die suddenly, I want you to go into the cave and use the funds I have left there for whatever need you have. Use it to fight Kyle and beat him. If you have to bring in an army, bring in an army. If this country has to be tamed by violence, then use violence. It's everybody's fight. It's going on all over the world. It's humanity against evil. This is just a skirmish, but you've got to win it."

"Don't figger. . . ."

"Let's go to bed," Hinton said wearily. "I've been thinking so hard this week I'm in a stupor."

Mack said nothing more about Hinton's coming to town. He shook hands with him the next morning and rode away. Once he looked back and lifted a hand in farewell. He had this last look at his friend, the feeling in him that he'd never see this strange, brilliant man alive again.

Chapter Seven

It was the middle of the afternoon when Mack reached Axe-handle. As he made the turn into Main Street, surprise jolted an audible exclamation from him. There were more people in town than he had ever seen before. Flags fluttered in the stiff afternoon breeze. Rigs and horses lined both sides of the street. Cattlemen from the west Sundowns and their families, dry farmers from the valley below Axehandle, townspeople: all of them stood in tight little knots along the boardwalk or shouldered their way through the crowd. Above the run of talk a baby lifted a hungry wail. A moment later the sound of it was lost in the brassy blare of a band playing "There'll Be A Hot Time In The Old Town Tonight."

Mack reined in at the stable. He asked the hosteler: "What's hit this place?"

"Celebration. Some big mogul from the railroad is here to make a speech."

Mack went along the runway and into the street. The band had stopped, and a bull voice roared into the sudden silence. "Speech-making about to start. Free coffee, compliments of Lou Kyle. This way, folks."

Lou Kyle wouldn't give coffee away if it didn't turn him a profit, Mack thought as he watched the slow drift of the crowd.

Dad Perrod, standing in the doorway of the feed store, saw him then and called lustily: "Come here, Mack." As Mack came up, he asked: "Where you been?"

"Having a vacation in the Sundowns." Mack grinned. "Don't ever go there for the ride. Hell of a poor country."

Perrod stepped aside and motioned for Mack to come in. "Look around, son, and see what you think."

Mack stepped in and, for a moment, could not believe what he saw. The store was empty. Even the sack of grain which had been Perrod's seat for so long was gone. An upended box stood in its place. Perrod's lips came away from toothless gums in a wide grin as he saw the look of blank amazement come into Mack's face. He said: "We ain't even got a forkful of hay left. Feller come in couple of days ago and bought everything we had. Didn't jaw about the price of nothing. Little better'n five hundred dollars it was. I put it all in the bank."

"Who was he?"

"Dunno." Perrod shrugged. "Never saw him before."

"My guess is he's buying for Kyle, and it'll go to the railroad for more'n we sold it."

"I kind of figgered that." Perrod shifted uncomfortably as if he expected a storm of anger to rise in Mack. "I didn't think about it right then, but they hauled everything over to Kyle's warehouse. That's a fact. I watched 'em."

"Mebbe I should have taken Kyle's offer." Mack stepped to the door and pulled the sign down. He stared at the board a moment and read aloud the words — **JARVIS FEED STORE** — his mind reaching back over the months to recall the promise it once had held. In a sudden gust of temper he split the board across his knee, threw the fragments the length of the empty room, and wheeled into the street.

Mack was hungry, and he wanted a shave and a bath, but at the moment he could have none of those things. Betty Grant's restaurant was closed. So was the barber shop. Mack drifted along the street and made the turn into the vacant lot where a platform had been erected. A great emptiness was in him that did not come entirely from hunger. He had five hundred dollars, but no feed store.

A stray cur slipped between Mack's long legs and ran on. A baby in a fat woman's arms began to whimper softly, and

Mack idly wondered if it was the same baby he'd heard when he'd first ridden into town. He stood there in the outer fringe of the crowd, a lanky, taciturn man with a week's dark stubble on his face and a layer of dust over him that added a somber gray tone to his shabby range clothes. His face held a gauntness, a tensity of purpose that was not usually a part of him. Inky Blair, seeing it as he moved toward his friend, stopped when he was ten feet away and waited.

Slowly Mack brought his mind back to focus on the scene before him. Lou Kyle was on the platform, a stocky, handsome man dressed in a black suit and white shirt, his black hair perfectly combed, his dark eyes flashing as he talked.

"This is the greatest day in Axehandle's history," Kyle was saying. "On this day we have the promise of the Pioneer Valley Railroad Company that steel will be laid into our fair city within a year, or eighteen months at the most. I do not need to tell you what this means. You folks who have pioneered this country know the resources that are here. You folks have blazed the way. You have taken the chances that all pioneers must take. Now it is fair and just for you to share in the profits that will come to Pioneer Valley with the building of the railroad."

Kyle spoke on at length, a flowery oration that contained, Mack said to himself, more hot air than facts. He saw Inky and moved over to him. "It's a hot wind from the desert today," he murmured.

"Yeah, I felt it, and I'm looking at the gent that's blowing it up," Inky said. "I'm wondering who's going to share in these profits besides friend Kyle."

Mack nodded.

Kyle was introducing the railroad man, a bald, heavy-featured man whose bony face was hideously ugly. Inky muttered: "Wonder where they found that?"

"They must have scraped the bottom of the barrel for sure," Mack answered.

"To Yance Bishop," Kyle was saying, "we owe the completion of the Pioneer Valley Railroad. For years we have been getting nothing but promises. Now the grading has started. Equipment and supplies are flowing in along the right-of-way in a great tide. Within a month the first steel will be laid out of Minter City. Ladies and gentlemen, our thanks to Yance Bishop."

A thunderous clapping rose from those next to the platform. It came, Mack saw, largely from the townsmen, Kyle's close following. Massive Tash Terris was there. So, too, was the hotel man, the manager of the Mercantile, Kyle's butcher, and a dozen more — all of them businessmen whose fortunes were closely tied up with Kyle's. Then Mack saw — and was surprised — that Cat Carne was with them. He stood, leaning against a juniper tree, his skinny body as relaxed as a purring cat's.

Little or no clapping came from the bulk of the audience. The dry farmers and the cowmen from the west Sundowns had been bled white by the high prices in the Mercantile or by exorbitant freight rates. It was natural that they should look with vast suspicion upon anything Kyle said or did. Mack, from where he stood, could not see Soogan Wade or Rosella. He asked Inky if they were there.

"They're in the crowd somewhere," Inky told him. "Soogan went home the day they buried Curly Isher, but Rosella stayed all week. Soogan rode back into town this morning with George Queen."

When the applause died, a great voice boomed from Yance Bishop.

"Ladies and gentlemen, I assure you it gives me great pleasure to bring you the good wishes of the Pioneer Valley

Railroad Company and to tell you that old promises are being kept this day. I want to congratulate you upon having in your midst a great man like Lou Kyle, a man whose heart and soul is in the building up of this community, a man whose vision goes far beyond the things that ordinary men like us can see. It is not to me you owe the completion of the Pioneer Valley Railroad. You owe everything to Lou Kyle who appeared before me and the rest of the railroad officials. It was Lou Kyle's persuasive tongue that convinced us we should take this action."

"He needs a pitchfork," Mack muttered, "to spread what he's spreading."

"He's knee-deep in it, all right," Inky whispered. "I'm not going to put this on the pages of the Axehandle *Weekly Times*. It would so corrupt the press it would never run."

"Today Axehandle has but a handful of people," Bishop was shouting. "Mister Kyle tells me there are not more than five hundred souls in all this end of the county. I venture to say that within a year Axehandle will have five thousand people. Lots will skyrocket. Men, if you have confidence in this country, you could make no better investment than to put your money into Axehandle property. Homesteaders will flock into the high desert. Wheat will grow where bunchgrass stands now as high as a horse's belly. They will plow up the bunchgrass. They will. . . ."

"The hell they will." George Queen's strident voice cut into Bishop's words. "That high desert is Tomahawk range, and it's gonna stay Tomahawk range. You bring in a bunch of sodbusters, and we'll hang 'em. By damn, we'll hang you with 'em."

"Shut up, George," Soogan bellowed.

Bishop pinned his gaze on Queen, a look of injured dignity upon his bony face. "Young man, I don't know you or anything about your Tomahawk, but I've built railroads all my life. I've helped make it possible for the homeseeker to come into our great West and till its fertile soil. I've seen arrogant and powerful cattle companies try to hold the settlers out. For a moment they have succeeded, but only for a moment. People come like an irresistible tide, sweeping everything before it. The desert blossoms like a rose. Wheat, man, wheat for mile upon mile, wheat to feed the hungry."

"Aw, hell," Queen howled. "How's a man gonna raise wheat in the desert? It's good grazing land, but it ain't wheat land."

"If it will grow bunchgrass, it will grow wheat. Now, if this ignorant fellow will permit me, I shall go on with my remarks. The railroad will bring wealth to this land such as none of you has foreseen in your wildest dreams. Within the next year fortunes will be made from the sale of hay and grain to the thousands of horses whose mighty muscles will lift dirt to a high, even grade between Axehandle and Minter City. You cattlemen will make a fortune from the sale of beef. The market for that beef will be in the stomach of every railroad laborer between here and Minter City."

"I can't stand it," Mack said. "I'm sick."

"I've got to stay and listen," Inky grumbled. "He might say something that has sense in it before he gets done."

"You're fooling yourself," Mack murmured as he turned away. "See you later."

Mack returned to the feed store, built a fire, and heated water. Before he had finished shaving, Dad Perrod came in.

"Where we gonna live?" Perrod asked. "Now that we ain't got nothing to sell and no chance to buy anything to sell, we ain't got a store. Looks to me like the bank will be taking the building back."

"We'll pitch a tent in the middle of Main Street."

"Fine idea." Perrod sliced a chew off his plug of tobacco.

"We'll put her right in front of Kyle's bank."

"I've been thinking of something else," Mack said slowly. He began stropping his razor, his forehead wrinkled in thought. "I'd counted on this feed store making us a stake which it didn't."

"Five hundred dollars," Perrod pointed out with pride. "With some luck at poker, you might step that up a little."

"I've got a better gamble. Had the notion while I was listening to that railroad windbag blow off. We can't sell horse feed, but looks to me like we could sell man feed. I was thinking about buying a bunch of steers from the little fellers in the Sundowns and driving 'em to some central place along the right-of-way. We could butcher 'em and peddle the beef."

"Good idea," Perrod agreed. "I've done lots of butchering. Between the hides and the meat, chances are we'd do pretty good. Better go see that windbag."

"I aim to," Mack said, "as soon as I can get at it. First, I'm going over to Betty's and get me a steak that'll reach from one end of my stomach to the other three times."

Mack finished shaving, put on a clean shirt, and cut across the street to Betty's restaurant. Apparently the speaking was over, for the crowd was eddying back along Main Street. Mack found one empty stool at the kitchen end of the counter. A moment later the full crest of the crowd hit the restaurant, wedged tightly in the door, and spilled out along the boardwalk.

"Steak?" Betty asked, pausing briefly in front of Mack, and, when he nodded, she went on into the kitchen.

Mack, watching Betty move swiftly and gracefully from customer to kitchen and back, suddenly realized that he had never really seen her before. She had been a shadow in the background of his mind, the picture of Rosella crowding her out. Now Mack saw her fully, her brown eyes, her hair so dark that it held a sheen in the glow of the lamp she had just lighted. She was short, a head shorter than Rosella, and she was pretty, but it was not a beauty as perfectly cast as Rosella's. There was a scattering of freckles on the tip of her nose, a long, white scar that ran above her left eyebrow.

"I'm a man of leisure," Mack said when she brought him his steak. "Dad sold everything out."

"I heard," Betty answered. "I wish I had a little more leisure."

"You're making your fortune."

"What good is a fortune?" Betty filled her arms with dirty dishes and disappeared into the kitchen.

When Mack had finished eating, he shouldered through the crowd, forcing his way to the street. There he paused, twisted a cigarette, and stood for a time, watching the crowd drift aimlessly. It was a good crowd with no great noise about it and no roughness. A group of women had gathered in the Mercantile to trade and visit with neighbors they seldom saw at home. Bits of their talk came to Mack about babies and socks and dinners for threshing crews. One said she hoped the railroad would get through this year, that she'd wanted to go to Portland for a long time, but that the trip was too long and too expensive by stage.

Early dusk had come upon the town, and lights bloomed along the street. Here and there rigs pulled away from the hitching racks. Horses' hoofs thundered pistol-sharp on the bridge that crossed Pioneer Creek as families took the valley road out of town. A poignancy struck sharply into Mack Jarvis as life eddied around him. This he wanted, a wife and children, a home, a solid and respected place in the community. Rosella was there in his mind again, centering this desire and refusing to go away. He threw his cigarette into the dust, walked rapidly to the hotel, and asked for Yance Bishop.

"Room twenty-two," the clerk said. "What did you think of Bishop's speech?"

"Hogwash," Mack said. "That *hombre*'s been so close to Kyle he's got some of the same smell on him."

Mack went swiftly up the stairs and past rooms sixteen and eighteen that Soogan Wade kept rented for the times when he and Rosella came to town. Mack found room twenty-two, knocked, and heard Cat Carne say loudly: "You're a fool, Bishop, for saying anything about beef in that speech of yours. Folks wouldn't have thought nothing about it if you'd kept your mug shut."

"Don't call me a fool," Bishop growled and walked heavily to the door. He opened it a bare six inches, his ugly face showing in the narrow crack. He stared at Mack, hostility stamped upon him. "What do you want?"

"I heard your talk this afternoon," Mack said, "and you mentioned something about delivering beef to the construction camps. I'd like to talk to you. . . ."

"That has been taken care of," Bishop said quickly and started to shut the door.

Mack put his shoulder to the door and shoved. Bishop, unprepared and entirely surprised by this maneuver, went back, lurched drunkenly for a moment, and fell, hitting the floor as hard as a man twice his weight. Mack came in, eyes raking the room. Cat Carne stood in a corner, a cigarette dangling from a corner of his lips, green eyes amused. Tash Terris sat on the bed beside Lou Kyle. The giant half rose, stared at Bishop, and then lifted his eyes to Mack. He straightened, his great hands raising to poise in front of him, his fingers spread.

"Want I should give it to him now, Boss?" Terris asked.

"Sit down," Kyle said testily. "I'm going to get a flock of chickens so you can wring their necks." He looked at Mack meaningly. "Tash is a great one to twist necks, Mack. He seems to have a yen to tie yours into a knot."

Bishop got up, swearing fiercely. He dusted himself off and said darkly: "I have a mind to have you arrested for breaking and entering."

Carne snickered. "He sure entered, and it kinda looked for a minute like he'd broken something the way you spilled out in a pile."

"Seems like I heard you say something in that big wind you raised," Mack said flatly, "about fortunes to be made, delivering beef to the camps. I could deliver that beef. I want to know why you won't talk business with me."

Bishop caught Kyle's eye, nodded, and said quickly: "I have just signed a contract with Mister Kyle for all the meat that our camps will need."

"I understand he was going to deliver all the horse feed you'll need, too."

"That's right."

"Why, you damned, lying robber," Mack exploded. "You were talking big about money for the people of this country. Looks like Kyle is the only 'people' that live here."

"We contract with men who have the financial backing and the moral integrity to deliver whatever their contract calls for."

"I can't say much about my financial backing," Mack said, his eyes narrowing, "but my moral integrity is a damned sight better'n this polecat you just signed up with."

Tash Terris rumbled an oath and started to get up. Kyle pulled the giant down. He said thickly: "You'd better go now, Jarvis."

Mack's grin was a quick, wicked slash across his face. "I heard you offered one thousand dollars to the gent who beefs me. Right, Lou?"

"It's a lie," Kyle snarled.

Cat Carne was on his feet, his skinny body loose, the smoke

from his cigarette a blue shadow before his face. He said: "I'm sorry I didn't plug you that day on the rim, Jarvis. Now I'm thinking I'll plug you before the night's over. You've got two hours to get out of town."

Mack looked at him, thinking there was no sense at all in this kind of a challenge, and wondering what lay behind it. Perhaps it was Cat Carne's bid for the death money Kyle had posted. Or it might be nothing more than Carne's desire to show off before important men like Bishop and Kyle. Or again — and Mack thought this must be the answer — Carne was only following Kyle's instructions. Mack said casually: "You scare me, Carne. I'm sure going to run . . . like hell."

Mack stepped back into the hall and closed the door.

Chapter Eight

Whether Rosella had opened her door, thinking it was Lou Kyle's step in the hall she had heard, or whether she knew it was Mack and wanted to talk to him was a question that Mack was never to have answered. She was standing in the doorway as he walked by, and, when he came opposite her, she said softly: "Come in, Mack. I've been wanting to see you."

He came in. Rosella closed the door and moved past him to stand beside the bureau. There was a lamp on it. By its light Mack saw the reality of a picture that was in his mind so much. The lamp put a glow upon her hair; her lips were full and red and expectant as if she knew she had the power to bring this man to her. She wore a string of pearls around her neck that made a startling contrast with the smooth tan of her throat. There was this moment when all the old hunger was in him again, this moment in which he realized more fully than ever how much his ambitions, the things in life that were important to him, were embodied in this girl.

He moved to her, put his arms about her, and looked into her face. He knew that they were remembering the same things, that she, too, was stirred by those memories. For a short time he held her that way, the old, sweet recklessness upon them. He was seeing her as she was when he had buckarooed for Tomahawk, when they had ridden together through the sage and tall bunchgrass. She had always worn Levi's and a man's shirt, and, when she rode against the wind, her hair had a way of fanning out into a crazy sort of halo.

There had been the time when they had ridden down the east slope of Pioneer Cañon to where Tomahawk cattle watered. They had stood beside the swift turmoil of the creek,

85

he had told her he loved her, and he had kissed her. She had said she could not marry him without Soogan's permission, but she would wait for him. The next day he'd drawn his pay, had come to town, and had bought the feed store.

The past lay hard upon them, forming a bond that held them together, and as suddenly was shattered into fragments that had no holding power at all. A broken promise was worse than no promise. She brought her hands up to his shoulders, and, as she did so, the lamplight fell upon her diamond, the sparkle of it bright and sharp and wicked. He stepped back and away from her, and watched disappointment shadow her face, watched the anger grow in her and bring its scarlet to her cheeks.

"What's the date?" he asked.

"We haven't agreed on it." She paused, setting herself now against him.

"There has not been a day in the past year when you have not been in my mind." He spread his hands as if trying to shove the thought of her away from him. "It's like a tree that's rooted there. It's grown so big it hides everything else, and the roots are so deep they won't come out."

"I'm glad." The anger had gone from her.

"Why should you be?"

"I don't know, except that it's hard to lose something that has been a part of you."

"Soogan sure was right. He said I'd never make a go of the store." Bitterness had its way with him. She had made no defense for herself. She could make none, and he wondered why he went on loving a woman who was promised to another man.

"I didn't want you to hear about it first from Lou. I wanted to tell you how it was."

But she did not tell him now. Instead, she turned and,

walking to a window, stood, staring into the street.

Mack was remembering the night she had ridden into his camp at Buck Spring. She had practically said she had made up her own mind, that it had not been her father's urging that had made her give her word to Kyle.

"I'd better mosey," Mack said.

Rosella turned. "I'm going to Tomahawk tomorrow." Her words were a frank invitation.

"Lou Kyle's your man," Mack said sharply. "Doesn't your promise to him mean any more than your promise to me?"

"Because I'm marrying him doesn't mean I'll never speak to another man," Rosella cried. "I'm not living in an Oriental country where a husband tells a woman what she can do or what she can't."

"I've got a hunch that you'll get a new slant on Lou Kyle after you've married him. Go ahead. Make a mess out of your life like you have mine."

"I haven't made a mess out of yours," she flared. "You seem to have developed an appetite for the food in the Top Notch."

"Been listening?"

"It's no secret."

"You care?"

"No. Why should I? She'll make you a good cook, and she'll be glad to get out of the restaurant where she has a hundred men a day. Go ahead and make a mess out of your life, Mack. Marry a girl who . . . who. . . ."

"I wouldn't say that."

"I didn't mean it that way," Rosella blazed. "But she isn't pretty."

"I thought she was." Mack started toward the door. There was no reason for this scene. He shouldn't have come in. He reached for the knob, but he didn't open the door. Someone was rapping a pair of heavy knuckles upon it. Mack whirled back to face Rosella. "Mebbe I'd better crawl under the bed until you get rid of him?"

"It's just like Lou," Rosella said and, stepping past Mack, opened the door.

It was Kyle. He looked at Mack, and anger laid a tight shine upon his face. "I didn't know you had company, Rosella."

"He was just leaving, Lou," Rosella said lightly.

"Are you ready?" Kyle asked. "I was talking business with Yance Bishop, and I forgot the time."

"I'm ready." She smiled at Mack. "We're having supper with some Axehandle people tonight. Who all will be there, Lou, besides Dad and Yance Bishop?"

"Jarvis wouldn't be interested." Kyle had stepped back into the hall and stood, waiting impatiently for Rosella.

Mack moved through the door and stood beside Kyle until Rosella joined them. She said: "I wish you were coming with us."

"I guess not," Mack said. "I heard about a bull that got into a kitchen once. He didn't fit."

Kyle moved to the stairs, keeping his broad back to Mack. Rosella smiled and, turning, took Kyle's arm. *It's foofaraw she likes*, Mack thought. *If that's what she wants, Kyle's the right man for her.* The bitterness of that thought was an acid in his brain. Kyle had the spit and polish; he had money. Rosella, looking to the years ahead, had bought what she wanted. Yet not once had she said she loved Kyle. It was a bargain she was not regretting, but still she wanted to keep Mack's love. She had made that plain.

Mack was still standing there when Kyle came back up the stairs. He did not speak until he was within three feet of Mack. When he did, his voice held a quality of wicked fury he had not let Rosella hear. "I've done everything I could to get you out of this country. There's nothing to hold you here now but the damn' fool pride of a stubborn man who wants to make a nuisance out of himself. I should have killed you a long time ago. When I found you in Rosella's room, I knew I'd waited too long. As long as you're alive, I'll only have half a woman. That isn't enough for me."

"That's a windy piece of gab, Kyle, just to tell me you're going to beef me."

"You get the point easy. If you're still around by morning, I'll know whether you believe what I'm telling you."

Mack laughed, the sound of it a slap across Kyle's wide face. "You know damned well I won't run. Ever since you got us into the Casino that time, so you could play big and make me look little, I knew we were going to wind up by smoking it out. It strikes me we've been wasting time."

Kyle shrugged his meaty shoulders. "It also strikes me that a man's a fool to stay in a place when it's more profitable to go somewhere else."

"You can't buy everything, Kyle. You can't buy Rosella's love, and, as for me, I figger I'll hang around to see that some folks get a square deal from you who haven't been in the habit of getting one."

"A man's life can be bought for a thousand dollars, Jarvis. You think that's a fair bargain?"

"If I had your idea of values," Mack agreed, "I'd say it was a good bargain. I'd even up it four bits."

"You think it's smart to hang around and get yourself a slug from an alley some dark night for nothing, just for what you call getting people a square deal?"

Jimmy Hinton had said: "It's everybody's fight. It's humanity against evil. This is just a skirmish, but you've got to win it." Mack thought about that. He could tell Kyle, but Kyle was not a man who would understand. So he said simply: "It's

89

smart enough to make me take that chance."

"Look, Jarvis." There was a desperation in Kyle's voice that was not like him. "The first decent thing that ever happened to me was falling in love with Rosella. You know I can do things for her you never could. If you love her, why in hell won't you get out of the country so she'll never see you again?"

"Because I don't think a coyote really takes off his skin and walks like a man," Mack said bluntly.

"I can make her happy if you aren't around for her to look at."

"You'll never make her happy unless you make her love you, and she'll never do that. It looks fine to her now, but give her a year, or five. Mebbe ten. Let her see what she's missed. It won't work, Kyle."

Kyle's face was cold and without expression. He said: "You won't be around to see. In a little over an hour Cat Carne will kill you."

Kyle left him then, moving swiftly down the stairs and across the lobby. Mack, thinking about Metolius Neele's saying it was worth a thousand dollars to kill him and about Cat Carne's challenge, wondered how far ahead this had been planned, and why Kyle had come back to make this last try at getting him out of the country. As he left the hotel, he saw the buggy that carried Rosella and Kyle make a turn at the end of the street and disappear. He should hate her, but he could not.

The crowd had thinned from the street. Mack moved along the boardwalk to Inky Blair's print shop, a strange confusion in him. Most of his life he had drifted. He had known his good times; he had taken what was his and had gone on. There was that streak of wildness in him. He had spoken to Kyle as if he were certain of himself and of what he had to do. He was not. He wasn't sure he even knew what he wanted. Perhaps the drifting life was his, the sky for a blanket, his saddle for a pillow, and purple twilight washing across the sage.

He came into Inky's shop, still thinking about it. He saw Inky look up from the desk where he sat, saw his friend's wide-lipped smile, and heard him say: "You just got here in time to read my editorial. Mister, I'm really going to lift the roof with this one."

Then Mack knew. He hated Lou Kyle for the things the man stood for and believed, the things he did to those who came under his power. But there were more important things to do than hate. One of those was to fight, and he had plenty of that to do. He winked at Inky as he reached for the paper. He said: "Have at her, boy. We've got a chore or two that needs doing."

Chapter Nine

Inky opened a cigar box and shoved it across the desk toward Mack. "Put one of those into your mouth and then bite hard so your teeth won't fall out while you read."

Mack sat down and reached for a cigar. He thumbed a match to life, and, when he had the cigar going, he asked: "What set you off?"

"Listening to that hogwash Kyle and Big Ugly put out this afternoon." Inky got up and began pacing the floor. "All that stuff about Axehandle's turning into a city and the lots skyrocketing. Hell's bells, nobody but Kyle owns the lots. Wouldn't surprise me any if he owned the damned railroad." He motioned to the paper in Mack's hands. "Go ahead and read it."

Mack took a fresh bite on his cigar, and cocked his feet on the desk.

For those in a community who stand for the long-range betterment of that community, who give of their time, their money, and their service, the Axehandle *Weekly Times* has nothing but praise. For those who claim to be public-spirited citizens, but in reality use every possible trick to extort money from the public, we have only the greatest condemnation. We refer specifically to Lou Kyle.

There are those who build a town, and there are those who destroy. Lou Kyle belongs to the latter group. It is not through lack of ability on his part, or lack of power and position. It is because he lacks a social conscience. As his schemes unfold, it is obvious that he has no thought for the welfare of the stockmen or the dry farmers. He does not think about the future welfare of our city. He does think of Lou Kyle and of those who stand with him and take his orders.

It is not for us to say that Lou Kyle has broken any laws. We have no evidence that he has. At this time we wish merely to point out that Axehandle's future lies in our collective hands. It is a job which calls for careful thinking and planning and perhaps the investment of every cent we have.

Undoubtedly Axehandle will be the terminus of the Pioneer Valley Railroad. The day is not far distant when a dam will be built on Pioneer Creek which will mean water for the valley. That, in turn, will make homes for thousands of people who are bound to look upon Axehandle as their trading center. Tomorrow's challenge is heard today. Shall Axehandle be a town with schools and churches and a park, a public-spirited town dedicated to serving those who live in it; or shall its reputation go out over the Northwest as a scheming, selfish, money-grabbing town, a place known as Lou Kyle's town?

Mack laid the paper down, a sudden tightening coming to his stomach muscles. He said softly: "Your sister's your only close relative, ain't she?"

Inky nodded. "Why?"

"Better give me her name and address."

"Why?"

Mack took the cigar out of his mouth. "Son, 'bout five minutes after Lou Kyle reads that you'll be getting a bad case of lead poisoning."

Inky stood spread-legged beside a type case, his fat face without color. He said evenly: "Mister, I'm scared. I'm so damned scared I don't even like sugar."

"Kyle's let you alone." Mack motioned toward the paper. "Why in hell are you bent on printing that?"

"You answer me a question first. Why hasn't Kyle bothered me?"

"Kyle ain't one to stir up a sleeping dog."

"That's it. He's let me alone because he figures I'm a walking hunk of fat with jelly for a backbone. The hell of it is he's right. Now I'm either going to fight, or quit looking at myself in the mirror."

Mack took his feet down from the desk, the front legs of his chair cracking hard against the floor. "I sure wouldn't keep you from fighting if that's the way you feel, but there is such a thing as going off half-cocked."

"I'm not going off half-cocked," Inky said indignantly. "I loaded that piece with enough dynamite to blow me out of Axehandle."

"Which is exactly what it would do," Mack said grimly, "but this ain't the time for it. Never waste your ace." He told Inky about what had happened at Jimmy Hinton's homestead, about his search through the east Sundowns, and about Yance Bishop's telling him that both the horse feed and beef contracts had been given to Kyle.

"They've already started grading between here and Minter City, and Kyle has sent several loads of meat to the camps, but I didn't know he had the contract." Inky shook his head in disgust. "But hell, we know Jimmy didn't steal Soogan's cows."

"Sure, but they've got to saddle somebody with it, and Jimmy's handy. Queen will get him, if we don't bust this theft and do it quick."

"A minute ago you were telling me I was going off half-cocked. Now you say we've got to bust this thing and do it quick."

"I'm telling you to hold that editorial until we get to the place where we want to stampede Kyle into the open."

"I'll hold it." Inky opened a desk drawer and dropped the editorial into it.

Mack leaned back in his chair, his eyes half closed as he thought about it. He said slowly: "We've got to make Kyle get out from undercover. If we sit pat, we're licked. Now, my idea is for you to worry him. Don't call a spade a spade. Act like a yellow jacket, buzzing in a man's ear."

"I'm not built like a yellow jacket, Mack."

"Try needling him a little bit," Mack went on as if he hadn't heard. "Write an editorial on what his freight monopoly's doing."

"I don't see what good it'll do," Inky grumbled.

"I don't know what good it'll do, either, but it will set folks to thinking." Mack rose from his chair. "If we had somebody with a little capital who'd risk it on a freight line between here and the Columbia, we'd really worry Kyle."

"Who's got any capital?"

"I've got a notion I can find it." Mack moved to the door, put his hand on the knob, and stood there a moment, his eyes on his friend, his thoughts a swift, chill stream. It was only a matter of minutes until he'd be facing Cat Carne's gun. He murmured, "Once you head out for some place, pardner, keep your eyes ahead. Don't ever look back."

"It was Lot's wife who looked back, wasn't it?"

"Never knew the lady."

Inky grinned. "It's from the Bible. That's why you don't know her."

"What happened to her?"

"She turned to salt."

"If it was you, you'd turn to sugar."

Mack went into the street and moved along the boardwalk past Betty's Top Notch restaurant. He felt the urge to go in, but did not. There was a freshness and a sweetness about the girl that might have been for him. Now, looking back with the keen insight that a man has when he knows he is standing close to death, he felt no regret. He had loved with the sort of love he had never known he could have for any girl before he had met Rosella.

Mack reached the end of the street and, pausing, looked along it. This town had been his home. It was the first time in his turbulent life that he had ever claimed a town as his home. Now he did not belong here. He felt it more keenly than he ever had before. He stood, pulling at the cigar, tasting it and enjoying its fragrance, and feeling suddenly the joy there was in living. There were so many good things in this life. The memory of them swept through him, and he wondered, as man has since the beginning of time, why there is so much misery and strife in a world that holds so much beauty.

Axehandle lay here before him, blanketed by night, Main Street a dusty path between two rows of stiff, false-fronted buildings. Along it, lights burst from windows of the Casino, the hotel, Inky Blair's print shop, Betty's restaurant. Here were common people, decent people who asked nothing of life but to be allowed to live and earn that which was by right theirs. Over it lay the shadow of one grasping, selfish man who schemed carefully and slowly and wickedly, and because there was little courage in this town, that scheming had gone unchallenged until now.

Kyle had not questioned Carne's ability to outdraw Mack and kill him. Mack realized, then, he had been letting his thoughts run along that same fatal pattern. In his own mind he was dead. "Don't ever look back." He had told Inky that,

96

yet now he found himself doing exactly the same thing. He was looking back along his life, thinking of Rosella Wade who would soon be Rosella Kyle, and closing the book of his future exactly as his romance with Rosella had been closed.

With a muttered oath Mack tore the cigar from his mouth and threw it into the dust. He drew his gun from the holster, gave the cylinder a quick whirl, and, with the Colt riding easily in the leather, turned and went again along the street. This was not the end. It was the beginning. Before it was finished, it would be Lou Kyle who would stand before Mack's gun and not one of his hirelings.

There were a dozen men in the Casino, most of them cowmen from the west Sundowns who knew Mack, from trading with him through the past year, and trusted him. They nodded when he came in, noted the gray grimness of his face, and held their silence. Mack strode past them and went on to the far end of the bar. There he turned, faced the batwings, and waited.

The barkeep came to where Mack stood. "What'll it be?" he asked.

"Nothing."

The barkeep nodded and returned to where he had been standing. Mack heard him say to one of the cowmen: "After looking at his face, I'd say somebody's got a date in hell."

The seconds ticked off in a slow, nerve-stretching rhythm. Time passed. This wait was like Cat Carne. He would set an hour and then be late, thinking he would crack his enemy's nerve.

It was thirty minutes after Mack had come into the Casino before the batwings opened and slapped shut behind Cat Carne. He came in to stand under an overhead lamp, its cone of light thrown downward, bringing out with striking sharpness the cat-like cruelty that was on his thin face. He stood there, slouched a little, all loose of joint, his green eyes making a swift study of the room and then fixing on Mack. He said: "I gave you two hours to get out of town. It's that and past, Jarvis. Why ain't you gone?"

Mack's grin was a quick and wicked streak across his dark face. He said: "I never obey the order of a smoke-eating gunslick, Carne. Besides, I aim to dig out the scheming son-of-a-bitch who paid you to kill me."

Then Mack stepped away from the bar and paced slowly toward Cat Carne.

Chapter Ten

A man at the bar cried out involuntarily and ducked around it. Others braced themselves and stood without motion. There was no talk and no noise but the indrawing and expelling of men's breaths. Behind the mahogany the barman coughed, the sound of it brittle and sharp against the quiet.

Cat Carne had expected to find Mack afraid. He had counted on the waiting to have snapped Mack's nerves. Now, seeing that his enemy was not afraid, that his self-control had not broken, he became possessed of a sudden and chilling thought that he might be the one to die. There was nothing on his skinny face to show it, nothing in his green eyes nor his cold exterior to tell Mack what Carne was thinking, yet he felt what was in the man, and he pressed his advantage.

"I had some respect for you the other day at your gate," Mack said in so low a voice that Carne had to strain his ears to hear. "Mebbe you figgered you had something to fight for, and a man's always got a right to fight for his own, but when you do another man's fighting, you're getting low enough to walk under your gate when it's closed without touching your hat on the bottom log."

It was then Mack deliberately took his eyes from Carne and threw a quick glance into the front corner of the saloon as if to signal a man standing there. Cat Carne, always a suspicious, questioning man, turned his head to look. In that same instant he drew his gun. He got in the first shot before Mack's gun was lifted from its casing and leveled, a clear shot that should have smashed life from Mack and did not because Carne's eyes were not on his target.

Then Mack's Colt spilled out a foot-long tongue of flame.

The bullet turned Carne partly around so that his second shot was as wild as his first. Mack fired again, the bullet driving into Carne's middle. Carne went back a single step, trying to keep his feet, trying to bring his gun up for a final shot, and failed. He reached behind him to a poker table for support, his hand wobbling uncertainly and, not finding it, he fell.

A gusty sigh rose from the men along the bar as if they had seen a thing they had hoped they would see and had not thought they would. The man behind the mahogany poked his head into view for a tentative look and, slowly, straightened.

Mack came to where Carne lay, his gun covering the fallen man. When he saw Carne's face, he wheeled away and went back to the bar where he had been standing when Carne had come in. He poured a drink and took it and stood there while a weakness came into him. These last hours had built to a peak. Now he was over it and going down the opposite side. Always it was this way after he had had a fight. The fury had gone out of him, the fire and the wickedness. He wondered when there would be a peace in his life, when he would not see death nor have the stink of powder smoke in his nostrils.

The medico had come and taken Carne's body. Inky Blair and Soogan Wade stood a yard from Mack, and, when he felt their presence, he motioned toward the bottle.

Natty Gordon had been talking to the men who had seen the fight. Now, moving toward Mack, he said: "They tell me you were waiting for Carne, and that he came and jumped you. That right?"

"Right," Mack poured another drink. "Disappointed?"

"No," Gordon answered quickly in the manner of one covering his real feelings, "but I'd like to know what this was all about. Personally, I'm glad to see Carne dead because he was a bad one. Three killings since I've been deputy up here, and every time he made the other *hombre* draw first. The boys say he got in the first shot and missed. Then you plugged him."

"His luck was bad. As to what's it's all about, I don't know. He told me I had two hours to get out of town. I ain't one to run, Natty."

"I reckon you ain't," Gordon admitted grudgingly. "Why did he tell you to get out of town?"

Mack shrugged. "I've got a notion which you wouldn't believe and I can't prove, so I'll keep it to myself."

"All right."

As the deputy started to turn away, Mack said: "Wait a minute, Natty. I want your help in the morning."

Gordon swung back. "What kind of help?"

"I want to get into Carne Cove. With you along it would be legal."

"That's a damned fool idea if I ever heard one," Gordon shrilled. "The Carnes don't want nobody monkeying around. After what you've just done to Cat, the other boys would plug you on sight."

"Mebbe," Mack admitted. "I'll take that chance. The point is they don't act like law-abiding people. If they were, why would they have been so damned ornery about keeping folks out?"

Gordon scratched his head. "I always wondered about it," he admitted, "but from what I hear, the old man was just cantankerous. Wanted to live by himself, so he homesteaded down there in a hole in the ground. I guess the boys took after him."

"There's something else to it besides being ornery. If there wasn't, why would they put up that log gate on the rim, and why would one of 'em stand guard all the time?"

"I've always had a notion," Wade cut in, "that those boogers were running an outlaw hideout."

"That's my hunch," Mack agreed. "Natty, you going with me or not?"

Gordon shook his head. "Not till I've got something definite to go on."

"Natty, you're the poorest excuse for a law officer I ever saw," Mack said angrily. "You're going with me, or I'll get me a handful of sand and pound it into your skull with the barrel of my Forty-Five. You could sure use a little grit."

Gordon swallowed, looked appealingly at Soogan, and nodded. "All right. In the morning." He made a quick turnabout and half ran from the saloon.

Wade watched him go, cursing steadily and fiercely. "No wonder nothing's done about my cows. One of these days I'm gonna take me a ride to the county seat and blacksnake that *hombre* who calls himself a sheriff. Why he keeps a no-good dude like Gordon down here as deputy is something I'd like to know."

"I've been wondering if mebbe Kyle was the reason," Mack said.

Soogan looked at him sharply. "Why should he be?"

"It was just an idea. It's politics somewhere."

"Maybe we ought to send for the sheriff," Inky said. "Chances are he doesn't know what's going on."

"He wouldn't come," Soogan grumbled. "He's fatter'n you are, Blair, and he sure don't like to ride."

Inky pinned his eyes on Mack. "That was good shooting tonight, son, but if I'd known you were going to swap smoke with him, I'd have been scared out of fifty good pounds."

"And if I'd known *that*," Mack said, "I'd have told you."

"You had no real reason to risk your hide fighting that gunslick," Inky growled.

"Sometimes you've got to skim the foam off before you can get at the stuff you want." Mack raised a hand to his face, fingertips rubbing the scar Metolius Neele had given him.

Inky, recognizing the gesture, said quickly: "Skimming the foam off is enough of a chore for one night."

"I reckon." Mack gave his friend a quick grin. "I kind of want this mess to jell so we can see what we've got."

"What kind of fool, beating-about-the-bush gab is this?" Wade shouted in outraged indignation. "You want me to pull out so you gents can talk personal?"

"I'm leaving, Soogan. I've got to go write about this shooting scrape before I forget how Carne looked." Inky started to move away, and then turned back. "I forgot to tell you, Mack, that, when you were gone, the Carnes started hauling hay into town to Kyle's warehouse. Awful small loads for some reason."

"Hell of a pull up that grade," Wade suggested.

"Graders have started moving dirt between here and Minter City," Inky went on, "and Kyle's sending beef to the camps. I saw a couple of loads go out yesterday. Left about dusk. Couple more went out tonight."

Mack nodded, watching Wade to see if Inky's talk made any sense to the old man, but he saw only a puzzled frown. When Inky had gone, Mack said: "Rosella told me you were eating with the top crust tonight."

"Naw," Wade grunted. "I'd make her ashamed. I don't know how to act in front of them people. I hear you ain't even supposed to drink your coffee out of your saucer. Reckon that's right?"

"Might be."

Mack drank his whiskey and pushed the bottle toward Wade. *The old man had aged a year in the last week,* Mack thought. Wade stood, toying with one of the coin buttons on his coat, his usual arrogant belligerence gone from him, his eyes on Mack as if he wanted to say something and was not sure he should.

Mack waited, knowing that presently Wade would talk, and after his third drink he did. "You've got guts, Mack. I wish you were riding for Tomahawk again. I sure could use a jigger who can handle a gun the way you can."

"I always had the notion you didn't hold much affection for me."

"I didn't like the way you hung around Rosella. Now that she's taken, I reckon you'll let her alone."

"You offering me a job?"

"Your store's a thing of the past," Wade said defensively. "I thought you'd be looking for a job."

"I need one, but I'm worth more'n thirty a month and beans, which same is a point I guess we don't agree on."

"Hell, I ain't gonna fire George Queen just to give you a good job."

"I don't want George's job. I want to find your cows, and I claim it's worth five hundred dollars."

"That's a deal," Wade said eagerly.

"There's one joker in the bargain, Soogan. You're gonna tell your boys to let Jimmy Hinton alone. He didn't steal your cows, and he ain't doing you no hurt."

"The hell he ain't," Wade bellowed. "He turned a spring into a stinking hog waller, didn't he?"

"That ain't enough to run a man out of his home," Mack said doggedly.

Wade held his silence for a time, a blunt finger tracing a tomahawk pattern on the bar top. Finally he said: "All right. I'll give you till fall. You better tell Hinton that, 'cause if you ain't found my cows and got the thieving coyotes in the calaboose who done it, I'm running him off the high desert if I have to do it myself."

"And you're going with Natty and me in the morning,

Soogan, just on the off chance we might see something in the cove."

"Sure, I'll go for the ride." Wade's eyes narrowed. "You hinting that my cows are in the cove?"

"Long as we're down there, we might as well look around. I've never been plumb to the bottom."

"I have," Wade said flatly. "You couldn't hide a week-old calf in the danged hole that you couldn't see from the rim. Get the idea out of your skull." Wade nodded and left the saloon.

It was then the cowmen moved toward Mack, and, when they had made a half circle around him, one said: "It ain't no secret you're bucking Kyle, Jarvis. We're in the same boat. Seems smart for us to get together."

"It would seem to be." Mack reached into his pocket for his paper and tobacco.

"Until the railroad comes," the man went on, "we're still paying whatever Kyle says we've got to pay for anything we get from the Columbia whether it's barbed wire or a barrel of flour. With him putting the squeeze on us through the bank, the railroad ain't gonna get here soon enough to do us any good."

"Go on." Mack shaped up his smoke, and returned the tobacco and papers to his pocket.

"Well, damn it," the man said, "we stand to lose everything we've got. Looks like Kyle's got us whipped."

"If we had our own freighting outfit, we'd lick him," Mack pointed out.

"No good." The spokesman shook his head. "There ain't nobody around here who'd put up the money to buy the wagons and teams we'd need."

"There is a way," the next man at the bar said. "I seen it done in Idaho once. Everybody who's buying forms a buyers' association. We delegate somebody like Jarvis here to do the trading, and the association pays him a salary."

"You've still got to have wagons and teams," the first man said doggedly. "You ain't gonna roll stuff uphill from the Columbia."

"We've all got wagons, we've got teams, and, by damn, I say it would be worth it to take enough time to go to the Columbia and back. Only thing is, we've got to have somebody who's done some buying. There's always a lot of little things most of us don't know anything about."

"You've been running a store, Jarvis," the first man said. "How about it?"

Mack nodded, not letting his face show the swift flow of elation that washed through him. "Sure, I'll take the job. Tomorrow morning I've got another chore to attend to, but I'll have Inky Blair run off some order sheets, and we'll fix up an agreement for you boys to sign. In a few days I'll make a swing through the Sundowns, and you can sign up. We could take the valley farmers in. If we're gonna hit Kyle, we might as well hit him hard enough to hurt."

They nodded — sun-darkened, bitter men who saw disaster running uncomfortably close. For a moment there was hope in them, and then it faded as they thought about Kyle, and the things he had done. One said: "When Kyle hears this, he'll come up with some dirty, damned scheme that'll fix us."

"Mebbe not," Mack said. "Any man can die."

"You as well as Kyle," the spokesman said.

"I'll look out for that." Mack nodded, made a way through the half circle, and went out of the saloon.

There was no light in the block now except that from the Casino. A cold wind, hurrying along the street from the Sundowns, sent a shiver down Mack's spine. Turning toward the feed store that was no longer a feed store, he wondered what

Kyle would say when he heard about the buyers' association. It might work, it might not, but it would worry Kyle, and for the moment that was enough.

They came at him from the darkness of an alley. How many of them he didn't know. They swarmed over him. He tried to get his gun and could not reach it. He struck out with his fists, felt flesh under his knuckles, and heard a man curse. Then something hit him on the head that took the light from his eyes and strength from his knees. He would have gone down if a great arm had not caught him. A voice said: "That's all, boys."

Mack did not know how much time had passed. He never went completely out. There was a whirling blackness streaked with red. He knew he was being carried, that later he was thrown to the floor, and a wall lamp was brought to life. Then the blackness fell away, like fog breaking suddenly from the earth and leaving the sun full upon it. He sat up, rubbed an aching head, and placed his back to the wall.

It was a single-room cabin, Mack saw. There was a bed at one end, the dirty blankets twisted into a gray, patternless mass. At the other end was a stove, table, and two chairs. Shades were pulled over the two windows. He had this glance before he saw the great figure of a man, sitting in the shadows next to the stove. A laugh rumbled from his throat. Mack tried to swing himself to his feet, but he had not the strength for it. He fell back against the wall, hopelessness pressing against his aching head. The man was Tash Terris.

Chapter Eleven

The big man rose from his seat beside the stove, shook his great body, and lumbered to the center of the cabin. He stood motionless for a moment, his beady eyes filled with triumph, meaty lips pulled away from yellow teeth in a wicked grin. He was like a man long hungry who, finding a meal spread before him, refrains from eating for a time so that the joy of anticipation can be prolonged. Mack, his head pressed against the wall, his hands palm down on the floor beside him, stared up into Tash Terris's brutal face and knew there was no hope for him.

"You killed Cat Carne tonight," Terris said harshly. "I don't like that."

"Nature makes funny friendships," Mack murmured.

"What do you mean by that smart talk?" Suspicion glittered in the man's tiny eyes.

"Let it go. I was just thinking."

"I said I didn't like you killing Cat."

"What did you think I was gonna do?" Mack demanded. "Stand there and let him plug me?"

"He told you to get out of town. You should've gone. Now you're gonna die."

Mack's brain had cleared, and his strength was coming back, but there never had been a day when he could have fought this creature with his fists and have expected to live. Terris's great hands would break him as easily as a single swing of a heavy sledge would smash a cracker barrel into kindling.

"Are you trying to tell me you're gonna beef me because I shot Cat Carne?"

"Yeah, that's what I'm gonna do. I'm gonna kill you dead."

"Hogwash! You're gonna kill me because Lou Kyle told

108

you to. He pays you ten dollars a month to do his dirty chores, and now you'll swing. You're a fool, Tash."

Terris pulled a foul-smelling pipe from his pocket and filled it. He was grinning broadly as if he knew he was outsmarting the man on the floor. He said: "I ain't got no rabbit brain, Jarvis. I'm smart. Just a hell of a lot smarter than you think I am."

"You don't act like it. If you were smart, you wouldn't do Kyle's dirty jobs. Go get him and have *him* salivate me."

"I'm gonna do the job myself," Terris said firmly. "Why should I go get Lou to do a job I like to do?"

"Because they'll hang somebody, and they'll know you've done the job because nobody else in the state can snap a man's neck like you can."

"That's where I'm smart." Terris had lighted his pipe, and now he leered at Mack, the smoke spreading its rank smell through the cabin. "I ain't gonna snap your neck. I'm gonna fool everybody." He went back to the stove and, picking up a length of pine limb, waved it at Mack. "I'm gonna take you down to the creek and crack your skull with this. Then I'll throw you in, and everybody will think you just got hurt and fell in."

It sounded more like Lou Kyle's scheming, Mack thought, *than it did an idea that would rise in Tash Terris's minuscule brain. It might work just about the way Kyle figured. People would suspect Mack had been murdered, but Kyle would have an alibi, and no one would suspect Terris of that kind of a crime.*

"You're still a fool," Mack said as if disgusted with the giant's reasoning. "There's no sense in murdering a man and taking a chance on getting strung up when you don't make anything out of it. Why don't you beef Kyle and take his money? He's got lots of it, and I'm broke."

"He'll pay me," Terris said slyly. "I tell you, I'm smart.

109

Lou wants you dead, so I'll kill you. He'll pay me for doing something I like."

There was no reasoning with that kind of logic, so Mack tried a different maneuver. He said: "Sure you're smart, Tash. That's what I've been saying. You're too smart to play another man's game. You ought to go into business for yourself."

"I ain't that smart. I listen to Lou, and he tells me what to do. He takes care of me. Lou's a good man." The pipe had gone out in Terris's mouth, and he dug a match from his pocket. "Why don't you get up and try to get away? You could make some fun for me."

In his own crude, animal-sly way Tash Terris was much like Cat Carne. Mack had not seen it before, but he did now, and in it he glimpsed a faint hope of escape. He had seen no gun in the cabin, nor was there any evidence that Terris had one on his body. He was not a man to be trusted with a gun, and probably Kyle had ordered him not to carry one. The nearest thing to a weapon was the axe, leaning against the wall at the end of the wood box, but it was just across the room from Mack, and he couldn't hope to reach it with Terris standing in front of him.

"You aiming to kill me here or by the creek?" Mack asked.

"I figgered I'd do it by the creek. Folks would suspicion me if they saw me lugging you down there. You see, I'm smart."

"You sure as hell are," Mack said admiringly. "If I had a brain like yours, I wouldn't be here."

Terris looked pleased. "You always thought I wasn't smart, didn't you? That's just 'cause we never knowed each other. I'm gonna be kind of sorry to bust you, Jarvis." He lifted a stove lid and knocked the dottle from his pipe. "Yes, sir, I'm gonna be kind of sorry." He came back to the middle of the room and pointed a ponderous finger at the door. "That ain't locked. Why don't you try to get away?"

110

"I couldn't get away from you." Mack looked at the door and quickly figured his chances. They weren't good. For all of Terris's huge bulk, he wasn't slow. Mack tried to raise himself to his feet and, pretending weakness, fell back against the wall. "You see, Tash, I haven't got it in me. I can't walk to the creek. Somebody'll see you lugging me, and you'll swing, and you'll know then just how smart you are."

Terris's low forehead furrowed in a frown. He paced toward the stove and back, the floor squeaking under his great weight. Mack's words had at last begun to have their effect. Terris put a hand to his throat, felt of it, and shook his head. "I wouldn't like to swing," he muttered.

"You wouldn't know much about it. They'd put you on a platform and tie a rope around your neck. Then they'd let a trap door go, and you'd be dead." Mack snapped his fingers. "Just like that. Put all your beef on a rope, and your spinal cord would pop before you could bounce twice. Of course, if the boys here in town strung you up, it wouldn't be that way. They'd just swing you from a juniper limb, and you'd strangle. You'd try to get your breath, but you couldn't. You'd be kicking and swinging and choking, and after a while you'd be dead."

"Lou wouldn't let 'em do that to me," Terris said. "He'd look out for me. He said he would." He put a hand to his throat again, felt around to the back of his neck, and slowly dropped his hand. "Sure, he'd see I got taken care of."

"He'd help 'em with the rope." Mack laughed scornfully. "Long as you're alive, you'd know why you killed me, and that'd help put a rope on Kyle's neck. If you were dead, he'd be safe. If he had any honest-to-hell guts, Tash, he wouldn't have you doing this chore for him."

Worry was in Terris now. It clogged his thought processes, drove him around the table in a nervous pacing, and set up a cross current of fear in his brain that added to the red haze already there. Then he seemed to quit thinking, his brain reverting to his original plan.

"Get up," Terris rumbled. "You're gonna walk down to the creek, and you're gonna get your brains knocked out, just like I said."

"Tash, you're sure fooling yourself about being smart. Before we get down to the creek, I'll yell my lungs out. I'll have everybody in town awake. Mebbe you'd better tear a piece off one of them blankets and put a gag in my mouth before we start."

"Yeah, guess I'd better do that." Terris plodded to the bed and tore a long strip from a dirty blanket. Then he straightened up, a new thought coming into his brain and setting up its disturbance there. "Why are you telling me what to do? If you open your mouth to holler, I'll hit you so hard. . . ."

Terris turned back to look at Mack, but Mack was not on the floor where the big man had left him. He'd reached the stove and had the axe in his hands before Terris saw him. The giant bellowed like a thwarted bull and came at Mack.

"Stand still," Mack shouted, "or I'll bust your head open."

But nothing could have stopped Tash Terris then. He rushed at Mack, huge hands outstretched, the feeling in him that somehow he had been fooled, but now he would have revenge for it. For an instant Mack did not move, standing as if rooted while he made up his mind. Terris, expecting to have a blow aimed at his head, raised one hairy arm in front of his face to ward off the axe. He kept the other arm in front of his chest, the hand balled into a club-like fist.

It was not possible to drive an effective blow past that huge arm. If Mack failed once, he'd never get another chance. Tash Terris, a monstrous, roaring fury, was death incarnate. So Mack, instead of holding his ground and swinging blindly for

Terris's head, stepped swiftly aside and brought the axe in a low, upswinging blow against the side of the giant's leg.

Terris hit the stove, crashed with it into the wall, and rolled off to the floor. The stove pipe broke loose and fell across Terris, soot streaming out of it and laying a black sprinkle over him. Terris rolled free, a steady roar of curses flowing from him. He came up on his good leg, threw his weight on the one Mack had struck, and fell forward, the cabin rocking with the weight of him.

Mack had reached the door, had tried to pull it open, and found that it was locked. Terris, in his childish seeking of fun, had lied to him. Mack had time to give the key a turn just as Terris fell the second time. Mack jerked the door open and whirled to face Terris. It was then that he saw the flow of blood, saw the agony on the giant's face, and knew he could safely and without trouble kill Terris. He said: "If I were in your boots, Tash, and you were in mine, you'd use this axe to split my head open."

Terris lay on his stomach, his head raised, a whimper of fear rumbling from him.

"Mack." It was a girl's voice, sweet and clear, and utterly unexpected. "Mack, are you all right?"

It was Betty Grant who stepped into the light, flowing through the open door. She carried a gun in her hand, and, when she heard Mack say, "I'm fine," she called, "Here he is, Dad."

"How did you happen to be out looking for me?" Mack demanded, his mind reaching back and seeing the horrible picture of what would have happened if he hadn't got in that crippling blow on Terris's leg and she had come just as Terris was leaving the cabin with him.

"I'll tell you later." She looked at Terris who had pulled himself to the door and quickly turned away.

Dad Perrod came into the light, and a moment later Inky Blair was there.

"We oughta let him bleed to death, but I guess we can't," Mack said. He took Perrod's shotgun from him, fired a blast into the night silence, and gave the gun back. "That'll bring 'em, Natty Gordon and the doc and the rest of 'em. Dad, you'd better stay around."

"Sure," Perrod agreed and slipped into the shadows.

As they followed an alley back toward town, Mack told them what had happened. Before they had reached the restaurant, they saw bobbing lanterns in the street and heard the shouted questions. Somebody yelled: "Tash Terris has got a leg damned near cut off."

"You gonna have Terris arrested?" Inky asked.

"No," Mack answered. "With that leg the way it is, he won't be bothering us for a while, and I'm kind of curious to see what he says about how he got it. Likewise, what Kyle will do now that two of his bully boys have petered out."

"He'll do plenty," Betty said bitterly as she unlocked her back door. "Come in."

"I'd better go on over to my place," Mack said.

"You're staying here with me tonight," Betty said. "Don't argue."

"I'm not staying here. . . ."

"Oh yes you are." Inky grinned. "You and Dad both. I came up a while ago and helped her fix a couple of beds in her attic."

"I don't care if you've got a dozen beds, I'm not. . . ."

Betty had lighted a lamp and had gone into her living room. She called nervously: "Come on in, Mack. You, too, Inky. I'll make some coffee."

Mack came in then, reluctantly, and watched Betty put the

114

lamp down and go into the kitchen. Inky paused to say something to her and then followed Mack into the living room. Inky said: "The girl's got a touch, hasn't she?"

"Yeah," Mack answered. He had never been in this room before. There were bright curtains at the windows, a sofa set against the wall, and a bowl of violets on the small oak stand. A cutting table and sewing machine stood together at the far end of the room, and on the table was a pile of filmy white cloth. That, Mack guessed, would be Rosella's wedding dress. He brought his eyes back to Inky and nodded. "Yeah, she's got a touch."

Mack sat down on the sofa, weariness coming upon him suddenly. He leaned his head against the wall and immediately went to sleep. When he woke, Dad Perrod had come in.

"A fellow'd think you'd do your sleeping in bed," Inky said with pretended indignation.

"Hush," Betty said sharply. She poured a cup of coffee and brought it to him. "Inky says you're going to the cove in the morning, so we won't keep you up long."

"What happened when the doc got there?" Mack asked Perrod.

"Nothing much." Perrod pulled a plug of tobacco from his pocket and reached for his knife. "Surprising little. Doc says Terris won't walk for a spell. Got a muscle cut." He shaved a chew off his plug and returned it to his pocket. "Funniest thing was how soon Kyle got there. I never saw a man look madder. Terris started to say something about a scrap, and Kyle says . . . 'You done it yourself. Don't try to say nothing else.' "

Mack nodded. "Gordon there?"

"Yep." Perrod opened a window and spat through it. "Yep, he sure was. Cussed a blue streak about being waked up in the middle of the night by a shotgun going off. Said it was

115

damned funny Tash had an axe cut on his leg instead of a load of buckshot."

Mack looked at Betty, thought about her searching for him in the night, a gun in her hand, and, when he spoke, his voice was more gentle than was his habit. "Why did you want Dad and me to sleep here?"

"Two reasons. The first one is that I'm scared. The second one is more important. You'll be safer here." When she saw the scowl darken his face, she added hastily: "I heard something tonight that gave me the biggest scare I ever had. I thought you were sleeping in the feed store, but by the time I had Dad awake, I guess they'd got their hands on you."

"What Kyle's done tonight," Inky said, "goes to prove that you can't beat him. He's got too many men and too much money to buy more. You've killed Cat Carne, and you've bunged Terris up so he won't bother you for a spell, and what the hell good is it?"

"I'm still alive."

"For the moment, but Kyle's showed his hand now. He aims to stop your clock for good. One of these days your luck is bound to run out."

"A man makes his own luck," Mack observed dryly. "Betty, what was it you heard?"

"Cat Carne, Tash Terris, and that railroad man, Bishop, came into the restaurant for some coffee. They talked so low I couldn't hear all they said, but I heard enough to know that they were sure you'd be dead before morning. Bishop said that if they failed twice, they wouldn't the third time."

"One was Cat Carne," Mack murmured, "and the second was Terris. What's their third ace?"

"It was something about burning your feed store building. Bishop said a crack on the skull would keep you from walking out, and everybody would think you had burned to death.

They'd been there about half an hour before Carne left. Then Bishop and Terris left when they heard the shooting."

Mack grinned wryly. "You know, Betty, it would be a pretty good world if it wasn't for the people in it."

Betty glanced at the cloth for the wedding dress and quickly brought her eyes away. "It *is* a good world in spite of the people."

"One gent like Kyle sure smells up the place," Inky growled. "He's a scab on the face of the community. Either some tough hand like Mack is around to pull it off, or folks get so used to it they just put up with its ugly look."

"Kyle's more'n a scab." Perrod raised the window and spat again. "This town's as near hell as any burg I ever seen." He slammed the window down and came back to his chair.

"I'll be sending you to The Dalles in a few days, Dad," Mack said. "Inky, tomorrow you run off some order blanks, long ones." He measured with his hands. "My job is to keep alive. I'm thinking it won't be long until Kyle schemes himself into a jackpot he can't get out of. Dad, let's go home."

"Mack, you can't," Betty cried.

"You stubborn, mule-headed ape," Inky raged. "Just because you're a fool for luck is no reason everybody else is. It's time somebody was busting that hard shell you've put around yourself."

They were on their feet, facing each other, Mack and Betty, a look in her dark eyes he could not read. She made a gesture, as if to hold him, and instantly brought her hands back. He saw then he had pushed her into a begging position, and the pride that was in her was too great to let her beg even from him. He said quite humbly: "We'll stay."

It was not yet full day when Soogan Wade and Natty Gordon ate breakfast with Mack in the restaurant. When they

117

rode out of town, the night chill was all around them. They reached the rim and, looking down upon the town, saw the fingers of smoke from newly made fires, standing like sedate, blue columns. Behind the Casino a man was chopping wood, the hollow echo of axe biting into pine rising to them.

"For once that burg looks peaceful," Natty Gordon growled. He laid a hostile glance on Mack's face. "That's 'cause you ain't down there."

"You've got no call to blame me," Mack said with sharp anger. "If you were a little piece of a lawman, we wouldn't be in the shape we are."

"And I'd have three hundred cows I don't have," Wade added.

"We're wasting time."

Gordon swung his horse and cracked the steel to him. The others followed.

The high, thin air still held its sharp bite when they reached the Carne gate. Gordon swung down and moved toward the end post to which the gate was locked. A shiver seized him, and, whether it came from the cold or fear, Mack could not tell. Gordon peered through the logs, trying to see the bottom of the cove, and muttered: "It's a hell of a long ways down there."

As he reached for the padlock, a Winchester laid apart the morning quiet with a sharp, echoing explosion, the bullet slapping into the post less than a foot from Gordon's hands. There was courage of a sort in Natty Gordon. He called: "This is the law you're shooting at, Carne. We want to go down into the cove for a look. If you refuse to let us in, I'll have no choice but to think that you're guilty as hell of something."

The man in the lava made no answer. There was a long run of silence, Natty Gordon watching the rifleman's hiding place with gray uncertainty, Mack and Wade sitting their saddles, eyes on Gordon. Presently there was the metallic rattle of wheels on rocks. Below the gate a man called: "Open up, Dan."

"Hold it," Carne called and carefully rose from the lava. He came warily to the gate, the Winchester carried at his hip, the muzzle of it swinging to cover Mack as if he thought neither Wade nor Gordon were worth watching.

Dan Carne was heavier and shorter than Cat had been, and his arms were thick and dark with a hair covering. His bulldog jaw gave an appearance of wideness to his face, and in that way he was utterly different in appearance than his younger brother, but his eyes were green and held the same cruel cunning that had marked Cat's. He unlocked the padlock and swung the gate back. A buggy wheeled through. Mack, staring at it in astonishment, saw that it was Lou Kyle's. The team was Kyle's matched bays; the driver was one of Kyle's freighters. He showed Mack a hard, expressionless stare, and drove on.

"All right," Carne said. "You boys can ride through, but the chances are you'll never come back."

Gordon ran a tongue over dry lips, his eyes flicking to Mack as if to see whether Mack had changed his mind about going down. He brought his gaze again to Carne. "I don't reckon you're as tough as you talk, Dan, but if we're going to stay here permanently, I hope you've got plenty of beef. The alfalfa I eat has got to come out from under a cowhide."

Carne jumped as if he'd been stung, his rifle barrel swinging toward Gordon, suspicion whetting his instinctive hatred close to the killing point. "What do you mean about plenty of beef?"

"I didn't mean nothing," Gordon said quickly. "I just like beef. That's all."

"Then go visit Wade. He's got lots of it." Carne shifted his Winchester to Mack. There was a gravelly quality about his voice that always made Mack think of two rocks being rubbed together. He stood motionless for a time, his green eyes filled with a shrewd and murderous appraisal. He seemed to be in doubt whether to kill Mack now or later. Apparently he decided to wait, for, as he stepped aside, he jerked a thumb down the steep, narrow road. "All right. Start out. If you make a wrong move, I'll put a window in your back."

They strung out along the road, Gordon in front, then Wade, and finally Mack. They came down swiftly to the cove floor, for it was a short road making a sharp pitch along the east wall of the cliff. Carne followed on foot, and, when they reached the bottom, he was but a few feet behind Mack's sorrel.

"Ride over to the house," Carne called.

It was obviously a womanless place. There were no flowers and no vegetable garden. Chickens and ducks were all over the yard, and from the barn a guinea hen set up her clattering. A black and white hound got to his feet, yawned, and sat down again, giving Mack a hungry look. Three mowers had been drawn up beside the barn, and Mack guessed that the alfalfa was ready for the first cutting.

They reined up close to the front door of the log house, Dan Carne still following. He said now, a murderous intent clearly marking his gravelly voice: "You gents think it's three to one, and, if you're lucky, one of you can get me before I get all three of you. You're wrong as hell. There's six men in that house. Before one of you could get a hand within two feet of your gun butt, you'd all be dead."

As if to punctuate Dan Carne's words, the ominous sound of guns coming to cock rode the still morning air.

Chapter Twelve

Natty Gordon pulled around in his saddle. "Look, Dan," he pleaded. "We didn't come down here for trouble. We just want to look around."

"Why?" Carne demanded.

"Well, Mack thought . . . well, damn it, Dan, . . . this has been a funny layout ever since your folks homesteaded here. It ain't natural. Your dad kept folks out of here, and now you boys been doing the same. It makes a fellow think something's wrong when you behave this way."

"I don't see nothing funny about it," Carne snarled. "If we want to live by ourselves, it sure ain't none of the law's business. It sure ain't the concern of no cowmen like old Soogan here, and as for that long-legged killing son-of-a-bitch" — he motioned at Mack with his rifle barrel — "it don't make no difference what he thinks 'cause he ain't gonna live long. Us Carnes stamp our own snakes, and we sure are gonna stamp that one."

"It was a fair fight," Gordon said quickly. "Cat forced him into it."

Dan spat contemptuously. "I don't believe it. All you town buzzards hold together."

"You put that Winchester down," Mack said, "and we'll see if you've got any better luck than Cat had on the draw."

"Nope." Carne shook his head. "I'll just drill you where you sit. Long as Wade and Gordon are along, guess I'd better drill them, too."

"Don't make a bad mistake like that," Gordon cried. "A lot of people know where we came."

"I'll shoot them other people when they show up," Carne

said casually and raised his rifle. "I guess I'll take Jarvis first. Where do you want it . . . in the brisket or between the eyes?"

It didn't make sense to Mack, but a lot of things had happened in the last weeks that hadn't made sense. Somehow all of it must fit into a logical pattern, and Mack thought there would come a time when he'd see it. Right now he was like a man who had gone to sleep and had started his nightmare in the middle. Dan Carne had the look of a person who meant to do exactly what he said, and it struck Mack that he'd be the cause of Natty Gordon's and Soogan Wade's deaths. He called desperately: "Dan, have you got any idea why we're here?"

Dan Carne lowered his rifle. "You're after Tash Terris, ain't you?"

"Terris?" Gordon shouted in vast surprise. "Why in hell would we want him? He hasn't done anything except try to cut his leg off with an axe."

Terris's presence here was as surprising to Mack as it was to Gordon, but he didn't let his face show it. "We aren't after Tash."

"Well, I'll be damned." Carne cuffed back his battered Stetson and scratched his head. "Then why in hell *are* you here?"

"Out of suspicion mostly," Mack answered.

"What have you been suspicioning about us?" Carne demanded.

"I've had several letters from the sheriff about the tough hands who drift north from Nevada," Gordon said, "and hole up somewhere. Leastwise they never get to the Columbia. Now we figgered you boys might be furnishing them a hideout."

"Well, we ain't," Carne snarled.

"Then who's the six men you've got in the house?" Mack asked.

122

"Hay hands." Carne leveled the rifle again. "I'm done talking."

Mack had expected this, and his hand was slicing downward for his gun when Lou Kyle said: "Hold it, Mack. Dan, put up that Winchester. You're acting like a fool."

Mack's fingers were wrapped around the gun handle, but he didn't draw it. Carne put down his rifle and cursed fiercely. He shouted: "Damn it, Kyle. Just because we've agreed to deliver hay and. . . ."

"Yes, I know what our agreement is."

Mack had shifted in the saddle and was watching Kyle who had come out of the house and stood on the porch. The big man was immaculately clad in a black suit, string tie, and white shirt. His hat was an expensive black Stetson. When he thrust his hands into his pants pockets, the skirt of his coat came back to show the silver-plated, pearl-handled gun that was cased in an elaborate holster. He stood there, wearing a cloak of amiability as easily as he wore his clothes, his white teeth showing in a friendly smile, and Mack, watching him, wondered what there was about the hay deal that would bring him into the cove.

A great sigh of relief came from Soogan Wade. "I'm sure glad to see you, Lou." He jabbed a finger at Mack. "That idiot brought us down here on a wild goose chase. Said we'd look around for my cows, and we damned near got our brains shot out of our skulls because of it."

Fear put a shadow on Dan Carne's face, and he reached for the .30-30 he had leaned against the porch. Again Mack's fingers were around his gun butt. He saw Kyle make a quick, warning gesture, saw Carne straighten up, and put his hands in his pockets.

Pete Carne came out of the house and stood beside Kyle. He was taller than Dan, and slimmer. His nose was both long and red; his eyes were bloodshot and furtive. He was a hard drinker, and his speech was heavy with whiskey now when he said: "I don't take to nobody calling me a cow thief, and I ain't gonna stand for it from the coyote who plugged Cat."

"There'll be a day for the settling of all debts, boys," Kyle said with mild persuasion. "This isn't it. Now, since these gents think there are cows in the cove that don't belong here, I suggest we let them take a look. Then they can ride and stay out. You boys aren't making any hay for me, standing around here auguring."

"Are you plumb lôco?" Dan Carne demanded.

There were bits of by-play here that Mack caught, inflections of voice, gestures, the exchange of signals between Kyle and Dan Carne, all building a conviction in Mack's mind that the stolen beef was in the cove and that Kyle was as deeply involved as the Carnes. These things Mack had noticed would escape both Wade and Gordon, for Wade was letting a slow anger come to a heat in him, and Gordon was too busy thinking about how to get out of the cove with his life to see anything else.

"We're willing to ride out now," Gordon was saying eagerly.

"No, Natty," Kyle was saying blandly. "For the sake of my friends, I want this accusation crammed back into the gullet of the man who made it. Did Jarvis accuse me of having a hand in the stealing of your cows, Soogan?"

"Well, no, I don't recollect that he did," Wade admitted. "He made a deal to find my cows and for me to let Jimmy Hinton alone, but I don't remember that he made mention of you."

"He's been trying to injure me since I announced Rosella's and my engagement," Kyle went on smoothly, "so I thought he might try to blacken my name along with the Carne brothers'."

"You're a cool one, Lou," Mack said, "and you're smart, but I've got a hunch you're so smart that you'll work yourself into a corner."

"We'll see who gets into the corner, my friend." Kyle nodded at Dan Carne. "Let's take these men past the barn and let them have their look."

"I ain't gonna stand for 'em snooping," Dan Carne said stubbornly. "You're getting hay here, and you're getting it cheap. . . ."

"I'm as interested in keeping them from tramping down alfalfa and grain as you are. We'll let them understand that the next time they show up, they'll get shot first and the talk will come later." Without waiting for Carne's permission, Kyle motioned to Mack and strode around the barn.

Mack turned his sorrel and rode after Kyle. Gordon followed, and after a moment's hesitation Wade came. Kyle had paused between a rye field and the barn, but before he could speak, Mack asked: "Why is Tash Terris here, Lou? You figger he might talk after he didn't make a go of it last night?"

A murderous rage swept Lou Kyle then. He snarled: "Jarvis, your luck's just about run out." Then he saw Wade coming, and he again took up the mask of bland courtesy. He pointed up the creek. "Look for yourselves, gentlemen. Dan tells me there is half a section of the finest hay land in Oregon in this valley. It's of lower altitude than the high desert, it's sheltered by the walls of the cañon, and the soil is rich. They take irrigation water from the creek and divert it over the land. Those are the reasons for them raising the tremendous alfalfa and grain crops they do. I might also point out that with such a place as the Carne boys have, it certainly would not be necessary for them to resort to stealing cattle or furnishing a hideout for outlaws."

"Always the showoff, ain't you, Lou?" Mack asked contemptuously. "There's something wrong here, and you know what it is, but Natty and Soogan wouldn't believe it if they saw it, so you don't need to spread it on a yard deep. That much ain't good for the soil."

"You see, Soogan?" Kyle spread his hands hopelessly. "I've saved his life, and now he accuses me. . . ."

"I'm not accusing you of anything," Mack cut in. "Not yet. All I want to do now is look."

"You've looked. Now ride out, and heaven help you if you ever show your face within sight of Carne Cove again." Kyle pointed to the road, slanting up the east wall like a thin knife blade laid alongside it. "You'd better ride. Dan's feeling plumb proddy."

Wade and Gordon wheeled their horses and rode back to the house.

"Just a minute," Mack said. He pointed to a long, spine-like ridge a mile up the creek that ran from the east rim to the cove floor. A man or a horse could follow that ridge from the rim to the bottom of the cove with far less difficulty than the road could be followed, but he did not make that observation aloud. Instead he asked: "Is there any land beyond that hog-back?"

"No," Kyle said quickly. "That's the north end of the cove."

Still Mack did not turn his sorrel to follow Gordon and Wade. He was thinking about what he'd said to Betty, that it would be a good world if it weren't for the people. Here was proof of it. The sun had tipped over the rim and was warming the last of the night chill. It lay brightly upon the alfalfa and grain in an eye-glittering brilliance and sowed diamonds on the white surface of the creek. It brought alive the greens and browns and yellows of the cañon walls. Here was beauty in a concentration such as Mack had never seen before, a master-piece of nature that made him feel as small as an undersized ant in the bottom of a giant coffee cup.

South of Mack and not far from where he sat his saddle the walls of the cañon so nearly touched that there was barely passage room for the creek. It ran in a swift and shouting turbulence that never saw the sun. North of the slanting hog-back Mack had noticed it would be the same, for he had seen it from the rim when he was in the east Sundowns. This tight little cañon, set off by itself from the world around it, was a perfect location for the execution of whatever lawless plans Kyle and the Carnes might have. Yet Mack was unable to see anything that would give him a clue to what those plans were.

"I'm giving you sixty seconds to get out of the cove," Dan Carne called.

"I can't hold him off any longer," Kyle warned.

As Mack turned his sorrel toward the east wall of the cove, he saw a long haystack set close to the base of the cliff. It was a carryover from the previous summer, browned by wind and rain, and Mack guessed that the hay being hauled to Kyle's warehouse in Axehandle was likely coming from this stack. It was nearly a mile from the buildings, and it struck Mack that there must be some reason for its being placed in that particular spot. Then he thought no more about it, for he had come up to Soogan Wade, and he saw the cold fury that was in the old cowman.

"You satisfied?" Wade demanded.

"No."

"Well, by hell," Wade raged, "what does it take to convince you? You can look down over the cove from the rim, and you can't see any cows. You're here and you still can't see any cows. You reckon Dan Carne's got 'em in the house?"

Kyle had come up now. He still held his air of pretended courtesy as he said: "Don't play your sixty seconds too close, Soogan, but there's one thing I would like to have you think about. Jarvis has tried to blame the Carne boys for a cattle steal. He has intimated I am involved. Can you think of a better way for a thief to shift suspicion from himself than to place it on somebody else?"

"It's a good trick," Mack said quickly, "and one you use right well."

Mack put his sorrel up the road that hung like a taut ribbon along the side of the cliff, his back a high, broad target. When he was through the gate, he stopped and waited for Gordon and Wade. He watched Kyle return to the house. A moment later Dan Carne started up the road to the log gate. Pete Carne and four other men moved toward the barn. Pete and one of his companions stopped to tinker with the mowers. The other three went into the barn.

"Come on," Natty Gordon said as he rode through the gate. "I feel kinda like I had a few coals of hellfire in my pocket."

As the three of them headed south toward the county road, Mack said: "Natty, you showed more guts than I thought you had."

"Thanks." The deputy glowed. "I'm plumb glad to get out of there with a whole hide instead of a hole in my hide, but I'd kinda like to go back down there sometime. There was a smell about that layout I didn't like."

"Hogwash!" Wade bellowed. "Damned fool hogwash! I didn't think you'd believe this stuff, Natty." He pointed a gnarled finger at Mack. "It gets too thick for me to swallow when you try to say Lou Kyle stole my beef. He's gonna be my son-in-law. Does it make sense for him to rob me?"

"He isn't in your family yet, Soogan. A lot of things might happen."

"They will if you can make 'em happen," Wade thundered. "George Queen thinks you and Hinton stole my cows, and now Kyle's got the same notion. I never took no stock in it, but it looks now like there might be something to it." He shook a fist under Mack's nose. "I ain't paying you no five hundred dollars, cows or no cows, and you'd better tell Hinton to vamoose. I ain't giving him till fall."

"I never knew you to break a promise, Soogan," Mack said softly.

"And if I get any kind of proof on you, Natty's gonna shove you into the calaboose." Wade wheeled his horse and put him into a dead run through the sagebrush.

"Reckon he don't like our company," Mack said.

Natty Gordon said nothing. Mack, glancing at him, saw that his face was hard and forbidding. The one moment in which he had shown some friendliness and a belief that there might be something wrong in the cove was gone. Natty Gordon might side against Kyle if he could thus gain favor with Soogan Wade. He was too much of a politician to buck both of them.

They rode in silence to the county road and made the turn toward Axehandle, Gordon staring ahead at the twin ruts that ran their twisting course through the sagebrush.

"All right, Natty," Mack said heavily. "You're nothing but a two-bit, chiseling politician, after all. You wouldn't have the guts to arrest Lou Kyle if you saw him commit ten crimes at once."

"You'll be in jail before Lou will," Gordon said darkly, "and I won't forget what you just said. It'll sure be a pleasure to turn a key on you."

Natty Gordon put his horse into a gallop, reached the rim, and dipped over it. Mack, riding slowly, watched the dust Gordon had raised drift away from the road and add its gray to the sagebrush and felt the bitter stab of disappointment. He had learned little of value, he had added to Natty Gordon's hatred of him, and Kyle's subtle accusation had raised a doubt in Wade's mind. It would have been better, he thought sourly, if he had done anything else than what he had done this day.

Chapter Thirteen

The sun lay bright and hot upon Axehandle when Mack left his sorrel in the stable and strode rapidly to the feed store building. He said to Perrod: "Dad, I'm going to take a swing into the west Sundowns to get this buyers' association rolling. When I get back, I'll have the orders. We'll know, then, whether the boys meant what they said last night. It'll take me a week. Soon as I hit town, you'll head out for The Dalles."

"Why don't you go?" Perrod asked.

"I'd be gone too long."

"You don't have no real hopes about this buyers' association, do you, son? It won't be no more'n a yellow jacket, buzzing in Kyle's ear."

"A yellow jacket gets plumb annoying, Dad. Get several of 'em working on Kyle at once, and mebbe he'll slap himself silly."

Perrod gave Mack a cool, studying look. "You find out anything in the cove?"

"No, but I've got a hunch. You keep an eye on Kyle's butcher shop while I'm gone. Count the steers they bring in and get some idea how much beef goes out to the railroad camps."

"You've got more than a hunch," Perrod said shrewdly.

Mack shook his head. "I did have till I got into the cove. Now, I'm worse off than I was."

There was a steady throb of restless energy in Mack that brought him along the street from the feed store building to the Mercantile and around the corner. Set in the back of the block were the buildings Kyle used for a slaughterhouse and an ice house. They were too small, Mack was thinking, for the amount of butchering that would be necessary to keep the railroad construction camps supplied. The ice house was large enough to preserve the small amount of meat necessary for the town trade, but it was far from adequate for the huge business Kyle would have through the hot summer months. It meant that there would be continuous butchering and hauling from Axehandle. Or Kyle might build a slaughterhouse somewhere along the right of way that would be more centrally located and haul directly from there. This seemed to Mack the most logical thing for Kyle to do, but apparently all the meat was being hauled from Axehandle.

Mack stepped up on the loading platform of Kyle's warehouse, but he didn't go in. A man came out of the gloom of the big building's interior, saw Mack, and gave a short, shrill whistle. He jerked up a Winchester from where it had been leaning against the wall and stood, watching Mack warily. Almost immediately a second man came out of the warehouse, a rifle in his hands. He said sharply: "Get out of here, Jarvis. No admittance to anybody not employed here, and especially you."

"I'm not trying to rob the place," Mack said irritably.

"Mebbe not, but you ain't coming a step farther. Boss's orders, and we'd get hell if we didn't enforce 'em. Go on now. Git."

"This is the way Kyle always runs his business?"

"He gave us the orders a little over a week ago. Now are you gonna go, or do you figger on making trouble?"

"I guess there's nothing in there for me," Mack said indifferently and walked away.

The parts of the puzzle were there, Mack thought as he turned toward Inky Blair's print shop, *all but one piece, and because that one piece was missing, the parts would not fall into place.*

Inky was setting type when Mack came in. He swung around

and, wiping a hand across his face, came to his desk. He asked: "Find anything in the cove?"

"Tash Terris is there. Lou Kyle is there. A bunch of men Dan Carne calls hay hands are there." Mack told him what had happened and added: "Practically a wasted trip."

Inky grinned. "Mister, sounds like you had quite a day."

"Something like that." Mack reached for a cigar. "These are free, I reckon."

"Help yourself." Inky waved a ponderous hand. "They don't cost anything for gents long on guts and short on savvy."

"That part about being short on savvy is sure me." Mack flipped the lid back on the box and took a cigar, but he didn't put it in his mouth. He rolled it between his fingers and began pacing the floor. "Inky, somewhere along the line my brain isn't working. It's all here. Everything I need to fix Kyle for good, but, by damn, I can't lay my hands on it."

"Keep working on it," Inky said somberly, "and you'll wind up dead. It's a wonder you aren't now."

"It is for a fact," Mack agreed. "Dan Carne was ready to let us have it, but Kyle was smarter. He figgered that once we'd had our look and hadn't found anything, I'd never get Gordon or Soogan down there again. Then he'd knock me off, and he'd be safe for the summer." Mack came back to the desk. "Soogan's cows are down there in the cove. I'd bet on it, Inky, but, damn it, I couldn't see 'em, and I couldn't see where they'd hide 'em. I've got a hunch Kyle is selling Tomahawk beef to the railroad, but how in hell is he doing it?"

"I never was any good on puzzles," Inky grunted. "You go ahead and wear your brain out. I'm saving mine."

"You're saving yours to rust. And another thing! Why is Kyle having the Carnes haul their hay into town? Why don't it go right out to the camps?"

"I dunno," Inky answered, "but I did hear that Kyle's

133

freighting horse feed up from the Columbia and taking it directly to the camps."

Mack jabbed the cigar into his coat pocket. "Something funny about this Carne hay then. Got those order blanks ready?"

Inky moved to the back of the print shop and returned with a bundle. "There you are, friend. Heading out in the morning?"

"This afternoon."

"There's a lot of nice spots for drygulching in the Sundowns."

"I've got a nose for 'em," Mack said. "So long."

Mack cruised along the boardwalk to the restaurant, saw Natty Gordon come out of the Casino and immediately go back, felt the growing hostility of the town, and heard a man say: "There goes a tough hand we could do without." Instinctively he glanced toward the window of Rosella's hotel room and wondered if she had gone back to Tomahawk. The thought of her brought a poignant stab to him, and he tried to put her from his mind. Still she lingered there, casting a dark shadow across his already dark mood. He found the restaurant empty, took a middle stool, and Betty, feeling the black run of his thoughts, waited in silence until he gave his order.

There was no satisfaction in the meal. When Mack had finished his pie and drained his second cup of coffee, he still felt an emptiness in him that no amount of food would ever fill. He drew the cigar from his pocket, smelled of it, and put it back. He looked at Betty and tried to grin, but the twist that came to his lips was crooked and without mirth. He said: "Not much fun in life lately, Betty. Mebbe we're working too hard, you filling men's stomachs and me doing nothing."

"Not much fun," the girl agreed. Her eyes were brown, and the laughter that was usually in them was gone.

"I'm going into the Sundowns," Mack said. "Why don't

you ride a ways with me? Lock the place up and let 'em starve."

"I have a woman helping me. She can run it."

"I'll get your mare," Mack said, and left the restaurant.

A load of hay was coming along the street. Dan Carne was driving the team. When he saw Mack, he drew his gun and laid it along his knees. Mack moved away from the front of the restaurant and stood with his back to an empty lot, his eyes on Carne.

When the wagon was opposite Mack, Carne pulled up. A sudden quiet had come to the street, a hush as people moved to windows and watched.

"Make your play," Mack said. "You've got an iron in your hand, and mine's in leather, but I'll bring you off that hay before we're done."

"If it hadn't been for Soogan Wade," Carne said darkly, "you'd be dead now. I didn't give a damn about that tin star packer you had with you, but I didn't want to beef Kyle's father-in-law."

"He ain't a father-in-law yet."

Carne jeered a laugh. "He will be, mister. He sure will be, and me and Pete will be there to dance at the wedding, but you won't. Between now and then Pete and me will have a date with you."

"Today's a good day."

"Not today. I've got a hunch you're fool enough to come snooping around the cove again. When you do, that'll be the day."

Carne spoke to his team then, and it seemed to Mack as he watched the horses strain into their collars that it was harder to start the wagon rolling again than it should have been. He called: "What've you got in that wagon besides hay? Lead mebbe?"

"Nothing here but hay," Carne said ominously and began

135

cursing his horses frantically.

Mack waited until the wagon had made the turn to the warehouse. Then he got his sorrel from the stable, told the hosteler to saddle Betty's mare, and rode after the wagon. It stood beside the platform, no one making any effort to unload it. Carne had already unhooked the team and driven it away. Mack reined up and studied the load for a moment, but he could see nothing unusual about it except that it was small. He swung down and, stooping, looked under the hay rack. It was then that the same two men who had stopped him on the loading platform came around the wagon.

"Jarvis," one of them said and patted his rifle, "I don't know why you're so bent on hanging around here, but if you keep it up, you're gonna get you some hot lead right in the brisket."

"I'm kind of interested in hay," Mack drawled. "You know I was in the feed business till I folded up."

"You'll fold up permanently if you don't get out and stay out of here," the Kyle man snarled.

"I'm on my way, but there's one thing I can't figger out. Never saw anything like it before." He pointed under the wagon to a steady dribble of water that had made a wet, black streak along the ground. "There seems to be a crack in the bottom of that hayrack. You reckon Dan Carne raised some hay that rains?"

The two men looked at each other, consternation sweeping across their stubbly faces. One of them swore and began to back away. The other one raised his rifle and thumbed back the hammer. He said darkly: "Don't tell Natty Gordon what you saw, or I'll hunt you to hell and back and plug you. That hay's sweating. Just sweating. Savvy?"

"Yeah, I savvy," Mack said and walked back to the stable, got Betty's mare, and led her to the restaurant. A moment later Betty came out, a shapely girl in her riding skirt with still, unsmiling lips. Color was in her cheeks, but it seemed to Mack that she was wearing a cloak of sober dignity today that covered the sweetness and the laughter that usually were so much a part of her.

"It's been a long time since I've had a ride." Betty stepped up. "Sometimes I wonder if the cost of making a living is worth it."

They turned toward the west Sundowns, rolling, pine-clad mountains that laid an irregular line along the horizon. They rode in silence until the town was behind them, Mack watching Betty and seeing the high way she held her head, the grace with which she rode. He said: "I never heard you talk like that before."

"Maybe I feel it more today. It seems to me we do the same thing over and over without getting anywhere. The woman who's helping me came in from Minter City. She likes it so well here she may buy the restaurant."

"You've made money, haven't you?"

"Money?" Betty said bitterly. "Yes, I've made money, for all the good it is. I don't have a need for it like you did."

This was a side of her he had not seen. He thought about it, the silence running on again between them.

An hour later they had climbed a long ridge and reached the first timber. Mack reined up. "Mebbe you'd better not go any farther. It'll be close to dusk before you get back."

"I need a stretch." Betty grimaced as she swung down. "I don't think I'll sit much tomorrow."

Mack twisted a cigarette and held a match flame to it, feeling the change that was in the girl, not understanding it, nor knowing why it had come. Dismounting, he pointed south to where the rimrock widened to make Pioneer Valley. "There'll be a lot of people here someday. Mebbe they'll look back on us and call us pioneers."

"Why don't they come now?"

"They're too soft. Somebody's got to tame a country. That's the chore we're doing. Always takes a few tough ones to plow the ground so the soft ones can plant the seeds."

"Where will you be when they come, Mack?"

"Why, I don't know. Tumbleweeds just roll with the wind till they hit a fence or something that holds 'em. Guess I'll probably be rolling."

"And you'll carry the same toughness with you that's in you now. Mack, I've seen you change. You don't laugh like you did. The town has turned against you. Lou Kyle has done that, and it's hurt you more than you have let yourself know."

It was true, and, knowing it, he did not argue. He said: "I guess it's no good to count on something too much. Mebbe it's better to let the wind carry you."

"No, Mack," she said fiercely, "but, when you've lost, there's no sense in letting your whole life be made bitter. You've killed a man and you've almost lost your own life in the last twenty-four hours. It will go on and on until you're dead. Must it be that way?"

"I reckon. After a while, mebbe, Lou Kyle will be dead. That would make the world a better place for a lot of people."

"I don't know," she said thoughtfully. "My folks were killed in the Piute-Bannock War. When it was over, some of our neighbors brought a bunch of captured Indians through the town where I lived. When they got into the mountains, they killed every prisoner. They said the Indians tried to escape, but I never believed it. Every one of the guards had lost some of his family in the fighting, and I think that was their way of getting revenge. But it didn't help. It didn't bring their people back."

"That's different. I'm not fighting Kyle just because he's busted me."

"I know." She laid a hand on his arm. "You're fighting for a principle, and, while you're fighting for that principle, you're becoming tough and hard. Don't change, Mack."

"It won't last forever," he said. "What about this business of selling out?"

"I don't know," she murmured. She moved away from him, her eyes on the valley, her lips tender and wistful, a hunger in her for a life she had never found. "After my folks were killed, some neighbors raised me. They weren't my folks, and I didn't belong to them. I just slept and ate in their house. I can't remember my own home very well, Mack. I guess a home is one of those things you dream about and never have."

He thought of Rosella and of his own dreams, and how they had centered around her. It would have been better if they had never met. If it had not been for an unkind fate, it would have been that way. But they had met. The longing for her was still in him, and to call himself a fool was no answer for it.

"It's a tough life if you're going to take what it gives you," he said a little roughly. "I've always taken what I wanted. Mebbe I'll have what I want before it's over."

"Are you sure you will still want it?"

Jimmy Hinton came to his mind then, and the question Jimmy had asked him. What would he do if Rosella saw her mistake in time and decided she'd rather marry him than Kyle? He'd told Jimmy he'd marry her today, if she said so. Now he wasn't sure. He said: "I never try swimming a river until I get to it." He turned back to his sorrel and stepped up. "I've got to move. I want to get back into the timber before I camp. Kyle throws a pretty long shadow."

"Be careful, Mack." That was all she said, but there was more to it than the words.

"I will," he said, "and don't sell out too soon. Dad's cooking ain't so good after sampling yours."

He grinned then, a wide-lipped, boyish grin that was more like the old Mack Jarvis. He raised his Stetson to her, a courteous, gallant gesture that came without thought. When he was deep in the timber and she was out of sight, he wondered idly if he had ever lifted his hat to Rosella. He couldn't remember that he ever had, but Lou Kyle did, and it would be one of the things Rosella would like. Kyle had ways that he did not. A man was what he was, and it was not in him to copy another. Then his mind came back to Betty, and he asked himself what there was about her that had brought that action from him. He searched himself and found no answer.

Chapter Fourteen

It took Mack a week to cover the Sundowns, and the blackness grew in him each day. Always it was the same. These men who had been in the Casino and had first made the proposition now wanted no part of the buyers' association. They wouldn't look at Mack when they talked to him. They were jumpy, and they were afraid. Kyle's long arm had reached from Axehandle here to the mountain wilderness.

It was difficult for Mack to wangle a full story out of any of them, but, when it came, it was almost the same from everyone. Jake Sigle had got to them ahead of Mack. By some miracle of communication Kyle had heard about the plan and had sent word to Sigle in time. He had told them that Kyle would give them more time on their loans, they could have credit at the Mercantile, and there was always a carefully veiled threat of reprisals if they tried to do business with Mack.

"Ain't it mighty damned funny Kyle would become such a big-hearted businessman overnight?" Mack would ask. "Kind of shows this buyers' association idea hit him where it hurt."

After he'd said that, they'd start looking across the clearing into the timber, or build a smoke, or perhaps pick up a pine limb and begin whittling. Cowardice was in them, and because of it shame was there. All of them knew it and felt it and showed a brusqueness that was not like them.

"It ain't really fair to buck him," they'd say finally. "He invested his money in this country, and just because he's got a pocketful of *dinero*, it don't prove he's out to slit our throats."

"You were mighty mad at him in town the other night," Mack would remind them.

"But he backed up soon as he heard what we were going

to do. He's given us what we want, and, as soon as the railroad gets into Axehandle, he's done as far as controlling how the freight rates go. Besides, we'd have to pay you something, and it'd take time for some of us to go to The Dalles." Then their eyes would lift to meet Mack's, and fear would be a naked thing in them. "Last year a man up on Bear Creek allowed he'd buck Kyle. Claimed he'd set up a store and freight his own stuff down. One night he got plugged between the eyes and his place burned. We've got families, Jarvis. We can't take no chances on that happening to us."

"Sure," Mack would say. "I see how it is."

Mack would step into saddle, and the cowman would call: "Stay for supper, Jarvis?"

"Thanks, but I'd better ride on."

Mack never made camp in the same place twice, and he seldom followed the road. He kept his fires small, and he put them out when he was done with them. He would sit quietly then, smoke, and stare up at the blue sky through a lacework of pine needles. He would think about the problems that faced him, and finally his mind would come back to Dan Carne's load of hay and the dribble of water that he had seen marking its line upon the ground. This made no sense at all, yet the feeling stayed in him that there was something important about it.

Each night it was the same. He would carefully examine everything that he knew, trying to see the pattern of Kyle's scheming, but it never quite came clear. Even if the Carnes were butchering Soogan Wade's cattle and hauling them to town under the hay, it would not account for the water he had seen under the wagon, and it would not explain how the Carnes could hide three hundred head of cattle in an area as small as the cove.

Mack did not hurry. It was his intention to see every cowman in the Sundowns, and he did not want to go back to Axehandle until at least a week had passed. There was the possibility he could catch Kyle off guard if he came back unexpectedly. Besides, there was the mystery of Jake Sigle, and, as Mack came closer to the summit and thereby closer to the town of Trumpet, the desire to see Sigle grew in him.

Sigle was Kyle's man, and that was something Mack had not known. It proved again, as it had been proved so many times to Mack, that there was no end to Lou Kyle's scheming, no end to his ambitions; that his legitimate businesses were cloaks to cover his lawless activities. Trumpet was Sigle's town. That much Mack knew, a tiny settlement atop the Sundowns where a man could find a room and meals and drinks when the rest of the state was too hot for him.

Mack came to Trumpet in the evening of the sixth day after he had left Axehandle. It lay between two mountains, the trail snaking on past to drop downgrade and eventually reach the Columbia. There was nothing much to the town: a rambling, barn-like structure that was hotel and saloon, a log barn and corrals behind the large building, and a half dozen cabins scattered haphazardly along the trail beyond the hotel.

Mack rode in cautiously, the knowledge pressing hard against him that he might be riding into a trap. He was taking a chance in doing something that would produce results of dubious value for him. Lou Kyle would not be here, and in all of Mack's thinking every trail led to Kyle. Still, and this thought drove Mack on when he might otherwise have turned back, Kyle had used Sigle to smash the buyers' association before it could get started. Sigle, then, must be a man high in Kyle's confidence, and, if he could be broken, a great deal could be learned from him.

Twilight lay all about in a thick blueness and gave to the sprawling town that strange mystery that comes to the earth as day slides into night. The mountains on both sides of the settlement rose in round perfection, standing close together and pinching Trumpet into its long, narrow shape.

Mack racked his sorrel and went into the saloon. A crude pine bar ran half the length of the south side. Two rickety poker tables stood along the opposite wall. There were cobwebs and filth and a great smell of evil about the place. *A man,* Mack thought, *would have to be in a bad way to hole up here.*

Mack crossed the room, the floor boards squeaking under his weight. Seeing no one, he moved around the bar and through the door into the hotel lobby. The desk was no more than a rude pine table, and there was as much filth here as in the saloon. Two broken-backed chairs were set close to the front windows. In the gloom behind the desk a paunchy man sat with his chair tilted back against the wall, his mouth open, his snores steady, discordant, and wheezy.

Mack pushed a toe under a front leg of the man's chair and lifted. The back legs scooted forward toward the desk, and the paunchy man hit the floor on his back, hard, the lamp on the desk rattling with the fall. He swallowed a snore on the way down, choked, and rolled over with a "What the hell?" Mack lighted the lamp and blew out the match as the paunchy one snarled: "It ain't dark yet. No use wasting coal oil."

Mack flipped the still smoking match at the man. It hit his cheek, rolled on down his fat neck, and brought a squall out of him. He batted it away, growled: "Tough, eh," and came to his feet, hand pulling a gun from a shoulder holster.

"Tough enough," Mack said, and hit him on the side of his head.

The paunchy man sat down again, his gun falling out of his hand. He stared up at Mack. He said: "Mebbe you *are* tough, mister. Who the hell are you?"

"You Jake Sigle?"

144

"Yeah, I'm Sigle. I asked who you were."

"Mack Jarvis."

Sigle got to his feet, jerked his chair upright, and sat down on it, his eyes covertly studying Mack. He said: "Let's go have a drink."

"I don't want your rotgut," Mack said. "I want information."

"Yeah?" Sigle laughed shortly. "I know plenty, friend, but most of it I wouldn't dare tell. When you run a place like this, you keep your mouth shut, or. . . ." He ran a forefinger along his throat.

"I'm not after that kind of information," Mack said. "I want to know what your tie-up with Kyle is."

Sigle felt of his face where Mack had hit him. His nose was flat and red, his mouth wide and thick of lip, his eyes small and wicked. He said: "I figgered that was what you wanted. Kind of spiked your fool buyers' association scheme, didn't I?"

"You did a good job," Mack grated. "That association would have hurt Kyle."

"So he had me spike it." Sigle's lips came away from his single yellow tooth in a grin. "And he kind of figgered you'd show up here soon as you found out who had done the job of spiking. In a place like this a thousand dollars is a pile of *dinero,* and he figgers you're worth that dead. That's why you're headed for boothill, mister. You're gonna be. . . ."

Mack sensed the play. He saw Sigle's eyes flick away from him toward the front door, felt the stiffening expectancy of the man, and the knowledge that death had come into the room ran a chill along his spine. He came around fast, pulling his gun as he moved, and dove sideways as he glimpsed the two men who had come in. A bullet splintered the door casing. Another breathed sharply along his cheek and slapped into the wall behind him. Then Mack had each man targeted, sent one

145

into a lurching fall with a bullet in his chest, and smashed the second one's right arm. The wounded gunman cursed shrilly, stooped, and reached with his left hand for the Colt he had dropped. Mack said: "Pick it up and I'll kill you."

The gunman straightened, his right arm dangling grotesquely, and began to curse again.

"Shut up and walk over here," Mack said. The man obeyed. "Why did you try for me?"

"One thousand dollars would have got us out of the country," the man answered.

"Who paid you a thousand dollars?"

The gunman nodded at Sigle, who still sat in his chair. "He would have. He was giving us free board for a week or more till you showed up. We was to keep out of the way and watch for a stranger. If we heard that talk he was giving you, we was to come in smoking."

"Kyle sure hired himself a polecat," Mack grated. "I oughta kill you, Sigle."

"Go ahead," Sigle said. "There'd be a lot of tough hands sore at you if you did. You'd have more trouble than Kyle's gonna give you." He got up and stepped around the desk, watching Mack closely. "I couldn't see why one jigger could give Kyle the jeebies like you have, but now that I've seen you, I know. Friend, you could do well working for the right people."

"I'll go on working for myself," Mack said. "How's Kyle getting Tomahawk beef out of Carne Cove?"

Sigle shook his head. "Damned if I know, friend. I don't worry about that end any. I've just got a working agreement with him to find a good man when he wants a killing done, but I sure missed this time. I didn't get men who were good enough. Not near good enough."

The wounded man whimpered: "You've gotta fix my busted arm, Sigle."

Outside the run of a horse on the trail came to Mack clearly. He listened a moment and saw hope break across Sigle's face. He said: "I'm going into the other room. Watch your tongue, Sigle. I'm not looking for more trouble, but if it comes, you can figger you'll have a chunk of it."

"Yeah, sure." The paunchy man bobbed his head. "I savvy."

"I gotta have my arm fixed," the wounded man groaned. "It hurts like hell. Stop palavering with the gunslick and fix it up!"

Mack slid through the door into the dining room. There was another door in the back, opening into a kitchen. Mack heard a man walk across the lobby and Sigle say: "Howdy, mister."

"How did this man get killed?" It was Natty Gordon's voice.

"Mack Jarvis just shot him," Sigle said. "These two huckleberries jumped Jarvis, but he got that one and busted this *hombre*'s arm."

There was a pause then, and Mack, watching through a crack in the door, saw Gordon scratch his cheek and stare at the dead man as if he could not make up his mind whether he wanted to say something more or not.

"Quite a ride from Axehandle, ain't it, just to ask about a dead man?" Sigle queried.

"Yeah," Gordon said slowly, "quite a ride." He looked at Sigle then. "Is Mack around now?"

"He's around. You want him?"

Gordon swallowed, looked at the dead man again, and said: "Yeah, that's why I'm here. He's wanted in Axehandle for stealing Tomahawk beef. We found a pile of Tomahawk hides in the back room of his feed store."

Chapter Fifteen

A club blow to Mack's middle would have had very nearly the same effect that Natty Gordon's words had on him. He recognized this play exactly for what it was. Kyle's efforts to have him killed had not panned out. This was a safer game. Kyle had planted the seeds of suspicion in both Soogan Wade's and Natty Gordon's minds when they were in the cove. George Queen had made no secret of his theories. It would be simple enough to smuggle a few hides into the feed store building and frame Mack. It was crazy and absurd, and any sane man would have seen through it, but Axehandle people weren't exactly sane when Lou Kyle called the turn. What was more, he could pull enough wires to send Mack to the Salem pen.

Mack, thinking swiftly of this, eased out through the kitchen and around the building to the front. He stepped into the lobby and said softly: "I hear you're looking for me, Natty."

The expression on the deputy's face would have made Mack laugh under other circumstances. He turned to face the door, carefully keeping his hands away from his gun.

Sigle snickered. "Go ahead and take him, star toter. I'll give you a free burying spot back on the mountain."

"You're under arrest, Mack," Gordon said, his voice too shrill to have the effect he sought. "Unbuckle your gun belt."

"If you want me, you can come after me," Mack taunted.

"Don't resist arrest," Gordon cried. "You'll just make it harder for yourself."

The wounded man whimpered, "Damn you, Sigle. Fix my arm."

"Natty," Mack said softly, "I don't think you're crooked. I think you're so damned anxious to hang onto your job that

148

you shut your eyes to what you oughta see, and shove whatever common sense you've got into the back of your brain. You know that, if I had stolen Tomahawk cows, I wouldn't be fool enough to leave their hides in my back room."

"They were covered up like you were trying to hide 'em till you had a chance to sell 'em," Natty said. "You fizzled out on your store, and you'll be needing some *dinero*. I'm not crazy enough to believe that you'd pass up a chance to make a few dollars on your steal."

"You're crazy if you do believe it. Kyle's trying to turn me into a corpse, Natty. If you want to make an arrest, why don't you take in Jake Sigle for putting a couple of gunhands onto me? Or that huckleberry who's bawling like a hungry yearling? Or mebbe Kyle himself. It oughta be a crime to pay a man to pull off a killing job."

Natty shot a glance at the grinning Sigle. Then he looked at Mack, and there was the appeal in his voice of one who knows he isn't man enough to do the job. "Mack, I'm not the one who tries you. I just pack the star, and I'm supposed to bring you in. The smart thing for you to do is come along without making trouble and stand trial."

Mack shook his head. "I wouldn't stand the chance of a snowflake in the desert, and you know it. I'm going back into the cove. When I find out how this steal is being worked, I'll get you, and you'll have a chance to use that star for the purpose it was intended."

"I'm not going back into the cove. You took me down there once on a wild goose chase."

Mack grinned sardonically. "You'll go, Natty. Now you ride back to Kyle and tell him not to send a boy to do a man's chore next time." He saw temper build in Gordon, saw the rose tint come to his cheeks, and knew that Gordon could be prodded to the place where he'd pull his gun. Not wanting to

149

kill the deputy, he said: "Take it easy, Natty, and don't try following me."

Mack went out the door in a quick, sideways movement and hit the saddle as he heard the wounded man's shrill cry: "I've gotta have this arm fixed, Sigle." Mack fired two quick shots into the front of the hotel and put his horse into a run. A moment later the forest darkness had hidden him.

Mack rode until dawn, then headed down a cañon to his right, and made camp. He slept most of the day. When he went on, he kept off the trail. He reined up occasionally, letting his ears keen the wind for the sound of pursuit. He was any man's target now. Up until this time his death would have been murder, but now he could be brought in across his saddle, and the killer could say the thief who had stolen Tomahawk cattle had died without telling what he'd done with them.

For the first time since Kyle had made the dramatic announcements in the Casino that had set into motion this sequence of violence, Mack could not see what his next step would be. It had been his plan to play a waiting game, knowing that, if he watched, sooner or later Kyle's greed would force him into making a wrong move. Now Mack could wait no longer. This had to be brought to a focus. Time had been on Mack's side, but it was on Kyle's now, and the tide was running out swiftly and mercilessly.

The sun was gone, and only the last lingering reminders of its light were upon the earth when Mack left the timber and rode across the sage-covered foothills to the rim. He reached it, saw the lights of Axehandle, the twisting, silver streak that was the creek, and came more warily down the narrow road and on into the town. Natty Gordon, he thought, was still behind him. It made no real difference with his plans whether Natty Gordon was in Axehandle or not. In any case, he didn't dare show himself. He had told Inky Blair his job was to stay alive. It was more than that now. He had to stay out of jail as well.

Mack left his sorrel in the willows alongside the creek above town. He followed the shadows toward Main Street, came across the littered alley to the back of his feed store building, and tried the back door. It was locked. The side window had shown a light. Dad Perrod was inside, or it was a trap. Mack thought about it a moment and, deciding it was a chance he had to take, knocked.

The door swung open. Perrod was standing there and looking along the alley. Mack said softly: "Blow the light out till I get inside."

Perrod acted as if he hadn't heard. He said loudly: "Aw, hell, someday I'll get me a club and bend it over that dog's skull if he don't quit making a ruckus out here." He shut the door, and presently the light went out.

Mack waited, knowing from Perrod's actions that Kyle had set a guard around the place. Then, hearing no movement, he carefully opened the door and slid in.

"Better not show a light," Perrod murmured. "I ain't sure he's got anybody in the alley, but he's had a couple of men watching from the street for the last two days. I reckon they figgered you'd ride in and rack your bronc in front. How'd you hear?"

"Got anything to eat?"

"I got some cold meat and biscuits. The coffee ain't real hot, but it's kind of warm. Can you eat in the dark?"

"I know where my mouth is," Mack said dryly. "Throw it together." He told Perrod what had happened and asked: "Is Natty back yet?"

"No," Perrod answered. "Kyle and Natty had quite a ruckus in the Casino last night, and Kyle allowed Natty wasn't much of a lawman. I'm guessing Natty went after you so, if he got the drop on you and brought you in, he'd be standing purty good with Kyle."

"That's about the size of it."

"Sounds like the buyers' association won't be much of a yellow jacket, buzzing in Kyle's ears."

"Won't have a stinger anyhow," Mack said. "Now what happened on this hide business?"

While Mack ate, Perrod gave him the story. "I never look in that danged storeroom. We ain't used it since we cleaned everything out the other day. I reckon some of them polecats must've come in when I was gone and left them hides in there. Anyhow, when Gordon showed up, he said he'd got word that there was some Tomahawk hides around here, and, seeing as I didn't figger there was any, I let him look without making no ruckus out of it. He nosed around considerable and turned 'em up in that storeroom. I'll bet he knowed where they were all the time."

"How many?"

"Four. They hadn't come off them cows very long ago, neither, so I guess whoever is doing the stealing is still at it."

"Fix a sack of grub, Dad," Mack said. "I'm going to ride out to Jimmy Hinton's."

While Dad busied himself with the grub, Mack twisted a smoke, cupping a hand over the flame as he lighted it. There was one job he wanted to do before he left town. He thought about it, estimating the risks and the probable gain, and knew it might, like the visit he'd paid Jake Sigle, turn out to be a wild play with more risk than the gain could possibly measure. By the time he had finished the cigarette, he had made up his mind. From now on the game would call for more than one wild play, and he'd take the risks as they came.

"Here's the grub." Perrod laid the sack on Mack's lap. "You're too danged stubborn to use your head, but from the way things are shaping up, you'd be smart to put some miles between you and Axehandle."

"I aim to. What'd you find out about Kyle's butchering?"

"He's hauling about fifteen beeves to the camps a day, near as I could tell," Perrod said, "and he ain't butchered that many by a damned sight. George Queen brought in one bunch a couple of days ago. About twenty-five steers, and that's all Kyle's bought on the hoof."

"Then even a stubborn galoot like Soogan could see what was going on," Mack said hotly.

"No, reckon he wouldn't. Them meat wagons go out in the night. There ain't nothing funny about it, 'cause that way he'd get the meat to the camps early in the morning. Wouldn't have it out in the sun. Been purty hot here this week, Mack."

"Keep your eyes peeled and don't light a lamp. I'm gonna call on friend Kyle before I leave town."

"That's a damn' fool play," Perrod said sharply. "What'll it make you?"

"Mebbe nothing more'n the satisfaction of punching him on the nose. Mebbe quite a bit more, if he's made out of what I think he is."

Perrod held his silence until Mack reached the back door. Then he said: "There's one thing, son. I didn't figger I'd tell you, but you're going off half-cocked anyhow, so I might as well."

Mack had his hand on the knob. He said: "What is it?"

"There was some graders in from one of the camps, and they was worked up about the meat they was getting. Claimed some of the boys had been sick from eating it, like mebbe it was spoiled. They was gonna quit till their boss told 'em they'd get good meat, and they'd have some pork before long to put a different taste in their mouths."

Jimmy Hinton had the only large number of hogs anywhere

along Pioneer Creek! That thought came first to Mack, and hard upon it was the second thought, that if the Carnes would steal beef from Soogan Wade to sell to Kyle, they'd steal pork from Jimmy Hinton.

"Reckon I'd better give Kyle his punch on the nose some other time," Mack said. He opened the door and slid out into the night.

Mack made a swing around the town and took the high desert road, the same road he had followed across Tomahawk range when he'd made his trip into the east Sundowns. He came again past the Carne gate, circling away from the road into the sage so he would not be seen, if a guard were posted there. He went on toward Round Butte and came again to the lava flow, the wildness of the black, twisted mass adding to the turbulence in his mind. There was a wildness upon the earth. It was in the wind and in the night sounds. Then, as always during these last weeks, his mind came to Rosella Wade, and the thought of her would not leave him.

There was no light in the window of Jimmy Hinton's cabin. It was late, yet Mack was remembering that the last time he came it had been late, and Jimmy was reading. Mack pulled up before he came out of the sage and sat motionless for a time, the cabin bulking darkly before him, trouble making a strong smell in his nostrils. He stepped down and moved cat-like toward the cabin. Again he paused before he came into the yard, plucked his gun out, and stood with his ears, keening the slow breeze for stray sounds, eyes strained to catch any movement that would break the stillness. There was none, yet the smell of trouble remained, as if death had come and let its black wings cease their fluttering while it kept its vigil, a somber link between life and eternity.

Mack came through the gate, stiffly and slowly as a man frozen. It was as if he knew what he would find, did not want to see it, but could not help himself. He was almost to the cabin when he saw the shapeless, black form on the ground, and what he had feared became a certainty. He struck a match and held it to the man's face. The dead man was Metolius Neele.

The flame traveled along the match, touched his fingers, and burned him. He let it drop and did not move, squatting there beside the cabin while his mind took cognizance of this thing he had seen and could not fully grasp it. Neele had been shot in the chest. His gun was still in his holster. Mack thought: *Jimmy didn't kill him. Jimmy couldn't kill any human being.*

Mack rose and called softly: "Jimmy." There was only a silence that ran on and on mockingly, a still night without sound except for the coyote calls from the Sundowns. He went on into the cabin, boot heels cracking pistol-like on the boards. He brought another match to life and held it in front of him, but blackness blanketed the flame, and he could see nothing. There was a lamp on the table, and he lighted it. He replaced the chimney and, stepping away, raised his eyes. Then he saw it, back in the shadows alongside the bunks. Jimmy Hinton's body was there, twisted and stiff. When Mack put a hand upon the wrist, he found that it was cold.

There was no emotion and no thought in Mack Jarvis then. He had felt this would happen when he had left Jimmy the last time, and he knew Jimmy had felt it. He knelt beside the body, and words came out of his mouth without conscious direction. "The dirty, killing sons-of-bitches! The dirty, killing sons-of-bitches!" Then he was aware that he was speaking, his voice sounding far away and strange to his ears, and he stopped.

He went back to the table and brought the lamp. He still wasn't thinking coherently, but the trail behind him was twisted and rough and sometimes shadowed with gunsmoke, and it had given him a training that set him to work now, looking for sign before he realized what he was consciously seeking. There was a bullet hole between Jimmy's eyes as perfectly-centered as if the killer had measured his head to find the spot into which he was to drive the slug, and it had been fired at close range.

Mack found no bullet holes in the wall. Nothing in the cabin was out of its regular order. If there had been any kind of a struggle, and the killer had attempted to replace things, Mack would have noticed, for Jimmy had always been a fastidious housekeeper, and there was one exact place for everything he owned.

Jimmy alone might have been killed by any of a dozen men. Mack thought first of the Carnes, because he remembered Jimmy's saying he was going to do some spying. If he had discovered the secret of the stolen cattle, this would be the answer Dan and Pete Carne would make, if they had known what he had been doing. But Metolius Neele, too, had been killed, and that added a factor, throwing everything out of focus.

Mack returned to Jimmy's body. He was lying on his side, right hand under him. Mack turned him over. In his hand was a gold coin with two small holes bored through it, the kind of button Soogan Wade wore on his coat.

Chapter Sixteen

The moments ran on, uncounted, while Mack stared at the coin button, and presently his mind gained a perspective on it. There could be but one explanation. Soogan Wade had shot Jimmy, and in his excitement had not known that Jimmy had flung out a hand and jerked the coin from Wade's coat as he had fallen. He had promised to wait until fall, and he hadn't. Then Mack remembered Wade's saying, after they'd left the cove, that he wasn't giving Jimmy until fall. *He hadn't,* Mack thought bitterly. *He hadn't given Jimmy more than a week.*

Mack pulled Neele's body into the house and shut the door. Then he mounted and rode south toward the Tomahawk ranch buildings. Soogan would be there or in town. In either case, he was going to jail, and Natty Gordon, politician that he was, could not overlook a clue like the gold coin button Mack carried in his pocket.

Mack rode through long hours of blackness and on past midnight, a single thought nagging steadily at his brain. *Jimmy Hinton was dead.* That was all, and his going had left a great emptiness in Mack that no one else would ever fill. He was a nester and an outsider, but Mack had liked him better than any other man he had ever known. He had come from a different world, yet somehow he had made himself fit into this wild and primitive wilderness. More than that, he had displayed a tenacious kind of courage that no other nester on the high desert had ever shown. Only a bullet could have removed him from the place he had taken for his home.

As long as he lived, Mack would never forget his last talk with Jimmy Hinton, and the change that had come over him. He had said: "It's everybody's fight. It's going on all over the

157

world. It's humanity against evil. This is just a skirmish, but you've got to win it." With only the glow of the stars above him, Mack swore to himself he would win this skirmish, and part of winning it was to bring Jimmy Hinton's murderer to a hangman's rope.

When he came at last to the Tomahawk ranch buildings, Mack paused, searching for a light and seeing none. Quiet was all about. The buildings sprawled in a dark, irregular pattern before him. It was familiar ground, and it struck him that it took a perverse fate to deal him this kind of a hand, to bring him on so grim an errand to the ranch where he'd worked, the ranch where he'd met Rosella.

Suddenly Mack realized that he had not thought about Rosella, had not considered how this thing he meant to do would affect her. It was the first time in many weeks that she had not been foremost in his mind. He had thought of Jimmy, and then of Soogan, and his mind had gone no further. Now he considered Rosella, but it made no difference. He could do nothing but go ahead.

Mack left his sorrel in a dry wash south of the ranch house, moved swiftly toward it, and through the locust trees in front. A dog came scurrying around the corner of the house, barking shrilly, and stopped when Mack said: "All right, Nip." He stepped across the porch, the screech of the boards under his feet terrifyingly loud, and went into the house.

Mack shut the door, dropped the bar, and paused to get his bearings. It was a log structure made out of jackpine brought from the Sundowns. There was a huge living room that ran the full width of the house except for a small corner that had been partitioned off to serve as an office. Soogan had his own bedroom in the back of the house, but he often slept on a couch in the office when he had worked late. Mack moved toward it now, wanting a look before he went on to the back.

During the years Mack had known Soogan and Rosella Wade, he had never once seen the slightest change in the arrangement of the furniture in the living room. There was a big handmade table in the center, the bear skins on the floor, the rack of weapons on the wall near the door, and a number of chairs covered with Navajo blankets Soogan had bought when he'd taken a trip through Arizona. Mack threaded his way through the furniture, slid into the office, and struck a match. Soogan was on a couch, a tattered quilt thrown over him.

Mack lighted a lamp, drawing his gun as he slipped the chimney into place, and lined the lamp on Soogan just as the old man threw back the quilt with a "What the hell?"

"No fast moves, Soogan," Mack said softly.

The old man swung his bare feet to the floor and sat up. He knuckled his eyes, shook his head, and slowly became aware of what was happening. "You danged, locoed fool," he bellowed. "What are you up to?"

Mack gave no answer for a moment. Soogan Wade made a comical figure in his drawers, gray hair awry, long, bony feet flat on the floor, his huge, untrimmed mustache drooping sadly around his mouth. Even his eyes were not as bright and sharp as usual, and the belligerent aggressiveness that had always dominated the old cowman was not in him now.

"Soogan, you've been tough and ornery in your day," Mack said, "but I never knew you to cold turkey a man like you did Jimmy Hinton."

A blankness came over Wade's lined face as his mind groped for the meaning of Mack's words. Then he said: "Son, I don't know what you're talking about."

"You killed Jimmy, and I'm taking you into town. I don't want trouble. If a lot of lead starts flying, we both might get hurt, and Rosella, too, mebbe."

"Put that iron up," Wade said testily. "I didn't beef Hinton."

Mack picked Wade's coat up from a chair and pointed to where frayed threads had once held a button. "Look at that, Soogan, and then look at what I found in Jimmy's hand. He'd been shot from up close, so he must have grabbed this as he went down."

Wade looked at the coat, then at the coin button, and raised his eyes to Mack. He said soberly: "Son, you and me have been on different sides for quite a spell now, but no matter what's happened, I've never lied to you. I'm telling you now I didn't kill Hinton."

"How are you gonna get around this button?" Mack demanded.

"I ain't gonna try. I don't know. All I know is I lost it several days ago. Last time I remember seeing it was when I was standing at the bar in the Casino, drinking with Lou. I got purty drunk. Mebbe I pulled it off myself. I sure can't remember."

"I never saw you drunk, Soogan. How come?"

"Well, me and Lou was gabbing about Rosella and the ranch. I was telling him how many cows we could run if we had the wells down and could get all the water we needed. I guess I just forgot to stop."

"Mebbe Kyle kept pushing 'em at you?"

"Yeah, he did. Kind of. Wanted to celebrate, he said." Wade paused, an angry frown lining his forehead. "What are you getting at, Mack?"

"I was thinking that mebbe Kyle pulled that button off to frame you," Mack said bluntly.

"I thought you was swinging around to that," Wade snapped. "I'm remembering they found some Tomahawk hides in your storeroom, Mack. Mebbe you and Hinton got into a

160

squabble over what you'd stole, and you plugged him yourself."

"You're too smart to believe that kind of planted evidence," Mack said thoughtfully, "and I should have been too smart to believe you beefed Jimmy. It begins to shape up now. I couldn't figger out about Metolius. Now that you've told me about drinking with Kyle. . . ."

"What about Metolius?" Wade demanded.

Mack told him what he'd found. He added: "Looks to me like Kyle and mebbe the Carne boys done the job."

"Metolius . . . dead." Wade said it as if he could not believe what he had heard.

"Dead enough."

Wade pointed a trembling finger at Mack. "Then it was you that salivated him. Everybody knows how you and Metolius felt about each other. Him and George both claimed you were the brains behind the outfit that's been stealing my beef. Metolius got the goods on you, caught up with you when you was there at Hinton's, and he got Hinton while you plugged him. That's the way it was."

"Hell, Soogan, use your head. You're thinking just like Kyle wants you to think. Mebbe he's got a reason for wanting you out of the way. He figgered I'd go off half-cocked, beef you, and make a run for it. I ain't made that way, Soogan."

"You hated Metolius, and he hated you," Wade cried. "He wanted to bust this steal because he said it'd give him a chance to square up with you. That's why he's been up there around the butte, watching things."

"Then chances are he found something that gave Kyle and the Carnes reason for beefing him."

"You got no reason to keep bringing Lou into this," Wade said angrily. "You're going to Axehandle yourself. If Natty Gordon never done anything in his life before, he's gonna do it now. You've got more'n a cow-stealing charge against you.

You're gonna hang for murdering Metolius Neele."

Wade got up and sat down again as Mack pronged back the hammer of his gun. He said coldly: "Soogan, there's no evidence to hook me up with shooting Metolius, but this button is something you can't augur yourself out of. Reckon a jury will decide whether Jimmy got it from you or Kyle. Now get on your pants, and let's ride."

"Dad won't be going with you, Mack. Drop your gun." Rosella stood in the doorway behind Mack, a small pistol in her hand.

Outside George Queen raised a great voice. "What's going on, Soogan? I heard Nip bark and some loud talk. Anything wrong?"

"Mack Jarvis is in here," Wade bellowed. "Smoke him out."

"It'll be a pleasure, Soogan," Queen yelled.

Mack heard the run of feet toward the front door and a pounding against it. As those sounds came to his ears, he was hard pressed by the knowledge that he was trapped. The odds against him were ten to one, and George Queen would find it a welcome task to burn him down.

Chapter Seventeen

Mack did not let his gun drop. Turning so that he could see Rosella and still watch Soogan, he said: "I didn't come here to hurt Soogan, but if you squeeze that trigger, he'll get hurt."

There was a calmness about Rosella Wade as she faced him that was almost serene. She had not lost her poise, but Mack knew she was thinking, and her conclusion would mean his life. Her eyes flicked once to the front door and came back to him. Her lips were tightly pressed.

"Drill him, girl," Soogan howled. "Damn it, go ahead and drill him."

Outside George Queen was pounding on the door and bellowing: "Open up. What in hell are you doing, Jarvis?"

"They'll kill you." Rosella jerked her head toward the door.

"Might be," Mack admitted. "Likewise some of those boys will get hurt for no good reason."

"I can't shoot him like this, Dad." Rosella moved swiftly to the door. "It's all right, George. I'll take care of Mack. You boys go back to the bunkhouse."

"The hell we will," Queen roared. "Open up, Rosella. You've got the ornery son that stole Tomahawk beef, and we'll take care of him ourselves."

Mack moved toward Rosella and put two quick shots through the top of the door. He said: "George, I'm pulling out. You try coming after me, and you'll get tagged."

"Come on." Rosella led Mack through the living room and into the hall behind it. "Why did you come here after Dad?"

"I thought he'd killed Jimmy Hinton, but I've got another notion about it now."

Rosella had closed the door leading into the living room.

They heard Soogan tramp across the room to the door and lift the bar, swearing in a steady, angry voice. "He just went out through the back, George. He ain't gone far. Don't do no shooting unless you see him. Rosella's with him."

"In here." Rosella opened a door and shoved Mack through. When Queen came into the hall, she was groaning and holding her head.

"Did that killer hurt you?" Queen demanded wrathfully.

"I was trying to hold him, and he hit me on the head."

"Where'd he go?"

Rosella groaned. "I don't know. He just went on."

"You're wasting time, damn it," Wade roared. "Go on. Go on. Chances are he's got a horse by now."

Queen raced on through the house, Wade and the rest of the men behind him.

"Watch it, boys. Either he got his horse, or he's hiding out here. Dark as a gut. He could be anywhere."

There was silence a moment. Then Queen asked: "What'd he come for, Soogan?"

"He was fixing to take me to town for killing Jimmy Hinton. He said Metolius was shot, too."

"Metolius?" Queen cried incredulously. "You sure?"

"That's what Mack said. Claimed he left the body in the cabin."

"We'll go fetch the body," Queen said heavily. "If we find Mack, we'll string him up to the nearest juniper we can find. There's a good chance we can pick him up, but I'll leave some of the boys here in case he's hiding. Keep your eyes open, Soogan."

Rosella slid into the room where she'd left Mack. She whispered, "What happened?"

Mack told her, and before he had finished, he heard the thunder of hoofs as the Tomahawk men left the yard. She was standing close to him in the darkness, the fragrance of her hair in his nostrils, the old hunger for her sweeping over him. He reached for her, put his arms around her, and she came to him willingly.

She whispered, "Mack, you'll never understand."

"I think I do," he said roughly, and let her go. For a moment he had forgotten. "I told Kyle he'd never buy your love, but mebbe he has. You made a deal, and I'm hoping it'll make you happy."

"I'll keep the deal I made," she said angrily. "You seem to have a way of making a fool of me, Mack. It happened in the hotel, and it's happened again. If a man once loved a woman. . . ."

"He goes on loving her, and he makes a bigger fool out of himself than she can ever make out of him. Why I still love you after you've promised yourself to a man for the cheap reason that he can buy the foofaraw you want is beyond me."

"I hate you," she flung at him. "I've saved your life, and you tell me that."

"Thanks for saving my hide. Mebbe we'll both feel better if we start hating each other. Now I reckon it's time to drift."

"Wait, Mack." She caught his arm. "I heard some talk between you and Dad I didn't understand, something about Lou using that button Dad lost to frame him."

"I can't prove it, but I think I will before this comes to an end. Now I've got. . . ."

"Mack, why should Lou want to frame Dad for anything?"

"Because if Soogan was dead, Lou would probably talk you into marrying him *pronto*. Then he'd be fixed with a mighty fine ranch."

"But he's got money, Mack."

"Mebbe so. He owns a lot of stuff, and he acts like he's got money, but suppose he needs some quick cash? It would

165

work out real well, him stealing cows from his future father-in-law. Nobody would suspect him."

"Are you done?" she asked calmly.

"Yeah, I reckon that's all. You wanted it, and you got it, and you're so danged stubborn, you'll go ahead believing Lou Kyle is a saint with little tin wings."

"I hate you."

"You said that before."

"It bears repeating. I wish I'd let George Queen and the boys have you."

"I'll be moseying. You sound like you really mean that."

This time she made no effort to hold him. Mack stepped into the hall and waited there a moment, listening. He heard nothing except Rosella's breathing, and even that slight indrawing and expelling of breath seemed to be telling him she hated him. He cat-footed along the hall into the living room, saw that it was empty, and moved through the front door. He went on a run across the porch and the yard, and somebody from the side of the house heard him, caught his shadowy figure, and opened up with a .45.

Mack raced through the locust trees, felt the breath of a slug that came uncomfortably close, and triggered three quick shots at the man who was firing. He ran on, angling sharply to his left, and reached the sorrel. He heard Soogan's hoarse bellow. "You let him get away! Get a horse. Bust the breeze after him."

Mack smiled grimly as he stepped into the saddle and swung his sorrel in a wide circle away from the house. Soogan Wade was a man in whom anger rose high and soon fell away. Later he'd be glad that on this night Mack did not die at his order.

The men George Queen had left at home had no great desire to get too close to Mack. They followed him for a time, and then turned back. It was early morning when Mack rode into Jimmy Hinton's yard. The Tomahawk men had come for Metolius Neele's body, and gone.

Mack found tools in the barn, and he took the morning to build a coffin, make a cross, and dig a grave behind the cabin. The hogs were gone. That much of the tip Dad Perrod had given him about the railroad graders being promised pork tied up. Jimmy's horse was still in the barn. Mack fed him and turned him loose. He made another search of the cabin, thinking he might find a clue in the daytime he had overlooked by lamplight, but he found nothing except a track of a flat-heeled shoe in the soft earth in front of the cabin. Lou Kyle, he remembered, never wore cowboy boots.

Sooner or later, George Queen would bring his riders back to the cabin in the hope of finding Mack there. Of that Mack was certain, for he knew Queen well. He understood the bulldog tenacity that was the strongest element in the man's character and the single-idea capacity of his brain. Mack, realizing how thin the time margin was for him, worked rapidly. He buried Jimmy Hinton and set the cross into the soft earth of the grave.

The first shock of finding Jimmy dead had gone from Mack. He was not a man to show his grief, but, as he stood now beside the grave, he felt more keenly than ever before the loneliness which had been in him since he was a child. There had been much about Jimmy he had not understood, but he knew, as he stood here in the early afternoon sunshine, that he would miss Jimmy Hinton as he had never missed a friend before in his life.

There was one more thing that had to be done, and Mack did it reluctantly, because it was a task he had never attempted before. He found a Bible among Jimmy's books and came back to the grave. Reaching into his memory to his childhood experiences in Sunday school, he thought of the Twenty-third

Psalm. He found it and read it aloud, haltingly, feeling the power and the promise of those lines:

> The Lord is my shepherd; I shall not want,
>   He maketh me to lie down in green pastures: He
>   leadeth me beside still waters.
> He restoreth my soul: he leadeth me in the paths of
>   righteousness for his name's sake.
> Yea, though I walk through the valley of the shadow of
> death, I will fear no evil: for thou art with me; thy rod
>   and thy staff they comfort me.
> Thou preparest a table before me in the presence of
>   mine enemies:
> thou anointest my head with oil; my cup runneth over.
> Surely goodness and mercy shall follow me all the
>   days of my life:
> and I will dwell in the house of the Lord for ever.

Then he looked up at the sky, and it was as if he were looking far beyond that blue bowl into the endless expanse of eternity. He said: "God, I sure ain't the one to be doing this, but nobody else is around. It won't make no difference with Jimmy, 'cause whatever scheme You got of taking care of folks after they cash in will be all right. He's the kind of gent You'll be looking out for." He paused for a moment, and then added: "But mebbe me saying this will make Jimmy feel a little better. He sure did have a rough time. Seemed like he was just starting to live when they plugged him, but I reckon he's happy now, because he knows all the answers to the questions nobody down here could give him. Amen."

Mack returned the Bible to where he had found it among the other books, and, taking a pair of binoculars down from the wall, he mounted, and rode away. He made a half circle of Round Butte and put his sorrel up its cinder-coated slope in easy switch-backs. Leaving his horse in the cap-like crater, he made his way on foot up the opposite inside slope until he could look down upon Hinton's cabin. Breath came out of him in a gusty sigh of relief. A half dozen horses stood in front of the cabin. Between them and the barn was a knot of Tomahawk riders.

Mack studied the Tomahawk men through the binoculars. Lanky George Queen was pointing toward Axehandle and evidently giving part of his crew their orders. Three of them nodded, mounted, and rode away, taking the trail Mack had always followed when he'd gone from Axehandle to Hinton's place. The rest of the outfit remained motionless for a moment, staring at the cabin, and talking as if greatly puzzled over something. Finally Queen motioned toward the horses. They stepped into saddles and rode back toward Tomahawk. A flat-lipped grin came to Mack's face. They had found the grave and knew he'd been there, but they couldn't decide where he'd gone.

Mack slid into the crater, crossed the rough, boulder-strewn bottom, and climbed the opposite side. He peered over, lying with his belly flat on the inside slope, and watched the Tomahawk men ride past the place where he had come up. A few minutes later they disappeared from view.

From where Mack lay, he could see Carne Cove, but he couldn't see the bottom. The crater was a perfect vantage point for him because he couldn't be seen from the desert. On the other hand, it lay spread before him in a far-flung panorama of sage and junipers and pine-covered mountains to the west and north. He saw the long crack that was Pioneer Cañon, widening only at the cove, and the desolate lava flow, twisting below him like a motionless, gray-black snake.

Mack didn't know what to expect, but he was convinced

that a period of consistent watching would turn up a vital clue. It was the lava flow that particularly interested him. He didn't know, and he didn't try to guess, the part it might have played in the disappearance of Soogan Wade's cattle, but it was the kind of terrain over which cattle could be driven without leaving tracks. If there was a secret entrance into the cove, the lava might well be the avenue the cattle had traveled.

For a long time Mack lay, studying the lava, first with the glasses, and then without them. It reminded him of a huge batch of fudge that had been spewed out of the butte's crater, had boiled down the side, and raced on across the desert to the rim of the cove where it had cooled, throwing up a wall along the lip of the cove ten feet high. It was this that puzzled Mack. No cow could climb a sheer lava wall, and that was exactly what the flow had made along the northern half of the cove's east rim.

The afternoon wore on, Mack keeping his position until it was finally dark. Occasionally small groups of Tomahawk cattle drifted around the base of the butte, and some moved toward the rim. They would, Mack knew, soon work back to the watering place on the creek or to some of the springs.

A feeling of desperation ran along Mack's tense nerves. The evidence he had all pointed to the one conclusion that the cove was the hiding place of Tomahawk cattle, yet the facts denied that same conclusion. He was as certain as he had ever been certain of anything that it was Lou Kyle's cunning brain which had planned this cattle steal. Now, as twilight came to the crater and flowed out across the desert, Mack marveled at the shrewd perfection of the plot. Apparently Kyle and the Carnes were taking no chance at all, for the scheme, whatever it was, seemed above detection.

When it was dark, Mack rode back to Hinton's cabin. He watered and fed his sorrel and left him in the barn. He went into the cabin, barred the door, and hung blankets over the windows before he lighted a lamp. Then he built a fire and cooked supper. There was another thing he had to do. Jimmy Hinton had told him to go into the cave below the cabin and use the funds that he had left there.

Mack studied the floor while he ate. *There must,* he thought, *be a trap door leading into the cave,* but he could see nothing indicating its location. When he had finished eating and had cleaned up the dishes, he worked his way across the floor, tapping and searching for a crack in the boards. It was several minutes before he found the trap door under one of the bunks. Prying it open, he held a match flame below the floor. The tiny blaze did little to light the pit-black interior of the cave, but it did show him that the rock bottom was not more than three or four feet below him.

Mack got up, propped the trap door open with a length of stove wood, and carried the lamp to the edge of the floor. He let himself into the cave and reached for the lamp. The cavern, he saw, was narrow and about twice the length of the cabin. The end into which he had dropped was shallow, but the floor tipped rapidly so that at the opposite end the cave was deeper than a man's head. The sides and floor were solid rock, but the lower end was filled with sand.

It was impossible to tell how far the passage went if the sand were removed, but, judging from the direction it ran, it might reach the cove. It was fantastic, but possible, that somewhere in the high desert a long cave such as this provided the passage by which the stolen cattle reached the cove. Mack, remembering the haystack close to the cliff, wondered if it screened the mouth of a cave.

This was a solution to the problem that had not occurred to Mack before, and for some time he gave it thought. Then he decided it wouldn't do. The cattle had been stolen weeks before. Neither Soogan nor George Queen knew exactly when. Perhaps it had been a slow dribble instead of a single steal. In any case, it wasn't possible to keep three hundred head of cattle in a cave until the railroad construction camps furnished a market.

Mack put this notion out of his mind until the time came when he could get into the cove and make the unhindered exploration he had wanted to when Natty Gordon and Soogan Wade had been with him. Holding the lamp, he began searching for the funds Jimmy had mentioned. He was more than three-quarters of the way around before he found it, a small, metal box set on a rock shelf within a few inches of the top of the cave.

Mack lifted the lamp to the floor of the cabin, laid the metal box beside it, and climbed out of the cave. Lowering the trap door, he carried the lamp and box to the table and sat down. He opened the box, and stared at the contents in surprise. There was no money in it. Only one sheet of paper and a key. Mack flattened the paper on the table and read:

Dear Mack:

You will find this only if I am dead, so this will be my last word to you. First, let me say that I understood Metolius Neele and George Queen better than you think I did. I also understood that you cut yourself away from them because you befriended me. That is something I have never forgotten, although I have found it hard to say to you.

Perhaps it is foolish for me to go ahead with my detective work. You might be caught and still get out. I wouldn't be able to, but still I've got to make the effort. After watching you make good men out of George Queen and his tough hands, I feel that I

must do something to prove to myself that I'm worthy of life in this country.

I have discovered part of the secret of the cove, and I hope what I am about to tell you will save you time and risk. What I have learned came from patient waiting and watching from the crater on Round Butte and from the rim inside the lava wall. I don't know whether Lou Kyle is involved or not, but tomorrow I'll find out because I'm going into the cove, and I'll find the one point which still eludes me. The cattle are taken from the high desert range through the lava wall. . . .

The brittle sound of breaking window glass brought Mack out of his chair. He drew his gun as he turned, but there was no time to fire. A hand jerked away the blanket from the window, and, as Mack's gun came up, a gun in the window flamed, the roar of its thunder loud in the small room. Mack did not hear it. A bullet splashing across the top of his head drove consciousness from him. He spilled out of his chair, falling full out upon the floor. There had been the awful sweep of knowledge pouring through him that he could not beat the gun in the window; then the black and bottomless pit opened up and claimed him.

Chapter Eighteen

A cold wind, blowing into the cabin through the open door and the shattered window, brought Mack to an aching consciousness. When he sat up, the cabin began to turn in a weird fashion, the walls moving toward him and retreating as the floor rose and fell in a rhythmical pattern. He closed his eyes and tried to remember what had happened.

It came back to him slowly, and with the memory was the feeling that, after he'd been shot, he'd heard more firing and the hoofbeats of running horses. Whether this was a nightmare that had come to him while he was unconscious or whether it had really happened was a question he couldn't decide.

When Mack reopened his eyes, the walls and floors of the cabin had regained their normal position and remained so. He pulled himself back into the chair where he had been sitting, looked into the metal box, and saw that both the key and Jimmy Hinton's letter were gone.

"Mack, are you all right?"

Betty Grant was standing in the doorway, worried and holding herself under a high tension. She was wearing her riding outfit, her green jacket buttoned tightly under her chin, and there was a gun on her hip. That was the picture Mack first caught, and he told himself he was out of his head. It couldn't be Betty. She wouldn't be out here on the high desert. She was back in Axehandle. She was asleep in her own bed where she belonged. This was no place for a girl, and, anyhow, she wouldn't be carrying a gun.

"You're hurt, Mack." She saw the trickle of blood on his forehead, and she came toward him swiftly, her cool fingers examining the wound. "It isn't deep."

Mack raised a hand to her shoulder. "I guess you're real. I thought I was still out of my head."

"I'm real enough, Mack. Sit still. Head wounds can be pretty tricky."

Betty closed the door and plugged the broken window with a wad of blanket. As she built up the fire, Mack asked: "How do you happen to be here?"

"Mostly because I got worried about you." She brought a pan of hot water and a cloth, washed the wound, doused it with whiskey she had found in the cupboard, and made a bandage for his head. "Now sit there for a while."

Mack twisted a cigarette, his eyes on the girl, seeing the sheen the lamplight put upon her dark hair and sensing the sweetness and the high courage that was in her. It was always Rosella who had been in his mind. The things she had done and said had made no difference. That was what love had meant to him, a tight and unchangeable power, holding a man and lasting as long as life was in him. Now, with Betty here before him, he felt the strength and steadfastness of her character, saw the beauty that it gave her.

Mack asked: "Why are you worrying about me?"

"Tomahawk men are in town, looking for you. So is Natty Gordon. They claim you killed Metolius Neele, and I was afraid you'd ride back into town."

"I wouldn't do that," he said grimly. "Not till I've settled my business with the Carne boys and Kyle."

"Who shot you?"

"I don't know. All I saw was a hand and a gun." He felt gingerly of his head. "I don't know whether that *hombre* aimed to kill me, or crease me like he done, but he sure fixed me up with a headache. Betty, I thought I heard some more shooting outside. Did I dream it?"

"No, you didn't dream it. I wasn't far from the cabin when

175

I heard the shot and saw the light in the window. Another man was on a horse, close to the porch. I circled into the sagebrush and started firing. The man who shot you had climbed in through the window. When he heard me, he came out through the door, jumped into the saddle, and both of them split the breeze, getting out of there."

"You shouldn't have done it," Mack said. "You might have been hurt."

"And, if I hadn't, you might have been killed."

"That's right." Mack pulled thoughtfully on his cigarette. "Wonder who that *hombre* was?"

"It looked like Kyle, but I couldn't be sure." Betty came to him, then, and laid a hand on his arm. "Whatever I did was a small thing alongside what you're doing. You can't keep on fighting alone, Mack."

"I've got some help from places I didn't expect, and that's a fact. If somebody hadn't got away with a letter Jimmy left me, I'd have had some more help. Mebbe I'd have found out all I need to know." He glanced at his watch. "It's quite a while till daylight. Now that you're on vacation, mebbe you'd like to cook."

She smiled. "Of course."

They left the cabin before dawn, and by the time morning twilight was flowing across the earth, they were inside Round Butte's crater, their eyes on the lava wall rising above the east rim.

"Not light enough yet to see much." Mack shifted so that he faced Betty. "You sell out yet?"

"No."

"Going to?"

"I think so."

"It's a sizable world," he said thoughtfully, "and I've got a hunch I'll be looking at some more of it before long." He stared at the rock wall. "Betty, am I seeing things, or is it the bad light?"

"I don't see anything," Betty said. "Just a lot of rock and sage."

Mack pointed with a forefinger. "See that notch, sort of a V?"

Betty studied the wall a moment and then picked up the glasses. "It's a V all right, but I don't see anything about it to get worked up over."

"Nothing except that it wasn't there yesterday," Mack said. "I spent the afternoon looking at that lava flow, and it didn't have any notch in it."

Betty handed him the glasses. "You'll have good light before long. Maybe it will disappear."

"I've seen some funny things," Mack muttered, "and a notch that shows up where there wasn't a notch is one of them. Now, if it disappears, I'll. . . ."

Mack had put the glasses to his eyes, and what he saw brought his words to an abrupt halt. A man was lifting a huge boulder and carrying it toward the notch. The light was still too thin to tell for sure, but Mack thought the man was Dan Carne. He handed the glasses to Betty. "Take a look."

Betty had her look, took the glasses from her eyes, and shook her head. "Mack, I've just seen something that couldn't have happened." She studied the wall through the glasses again before she gave them back to Mack. "See if you can find the notch now."

Mack looked for a long moment, moving his glasses so that he brought the entire length of the wall into his vision. "It isn't there," he said in awe. "What did you see when I first gave them to you?"

"I saw a man carrying a boulder that was as big as a house, but it isn't possible, Mack. Hercules couldn't have done it."

"Funny thing." Mack cuffed back his Stetson and scratched his head thoughtfully. "Sure is a funny thing. I don't know that Hercules *hombre*, but I reckon he ain't siding the Carne boys."

"What's funny?"

"Why, I saw a man carrying a boulder as big as a house, and I know it ain't possible."

"This is like being in a country where the law of gravity isn't working," Betty said breathlessly. "Do you think we're crazy?"

"I might be after getting that slug along my skull," Mack conceded, "but you're not, and I don't reckon Congress has repealed the law of gravity." He stood up and slipped the glasses into their case. "I'm going to take a closer look. Mebbe you'd better light out for town."

"No," Betty said flatly. "Not till I find out what kind of a strong man we have in these parts."

They rode down the east slope of the butte, circled back to the west side, and followed the lava flow until they reached the spot where they had seen the notch. Mack reined up and stepped down. He looked up at Betty, worry bringing a deep-furrowed frown to his forehead. He said in a low tone: "Betty, this game is for keeps, and if I'm reading the sign right, I'm going to have a look at Kyle's hole card before long."

"And men like Kyle and the Carne boys would just as soon add another killing or so to the ones they've already done since they can only hang once anyhow."

"That's right. So keep your voice down. One of Kyle's tough hands might be close enough to hear us."

She dismounted then and stood, facing Mack, a slim-bodied, shapely girl whose brown eyes met his squarely. "I don't care who's around here. I won't go back until I know what's happening."

178

"All right." Mack's grin was a quick flash across his bronze face. "I know better than to argue with a woman when she uses that tone. Let's see what we can figger out."

Betty watched in silence while Mack made a careful examination of the lava wall. It was mid-morning before he whistled softly and stepped back from the lava to view it at a greater distance. "Pretty smart *hombres*," he said softly. "If we hadn't spotted that jigger through the glass, we'd have hunted along here all summer and not found this."

"I don't see that we've found anything," Betty said skeptically. "Looks like lava rock to me."

"Which is exactly what they wanted us to think. Looks to me like they lift this out at night and put it back about dawn. Some time during the night they chouse a few cows through, or mebbe the critters drift through." Mack shook his head in admiration. "Yes, sir, this is a smart job even for a cute *hombre* like Lou Kyle."

"Will you tell me what you're talking about?" Betty demanded in exasperation.

"Rub your hand across this chunk of lava and then on over to here."

Betty obeyed and wheeled to face Mack. "Why, this is soft here. It's . . . Mack, it's pumice. Pumice wouldn't be here like that. Not in a. . . ." She turned back to the lava, fingers searching for the edge of the pumice plug. "I'll bet I could lift that thing myself."

"Just like lifting air. You probably could hoist that chunk all right, but don't do it now."

"Why not?"

"I have an idea Jimmy pulled it out and got drilled for his trouble." Mack drew papers and tobacco from his pocket. "Chances are Kyle and the Carnes were plumb proddy after Jimmy found out what their game was. If we start playing around, we'll get a chunk of lead where it'll hurt."

"But if Jimmy . . . ?"

"Mebbe they didn't have a guard out here then." Mack looked at his cigarette and reluctantly threw it away. "Reckon I'd better not smoke." He motioned toward the lava wall. "Kyle and the Carnes likely figgered this was so slick nobody would ever stumble onto it, but after Jimmy did, they'll be worried enough to keep a man on guard."

"I'd like to see what's on the other side of this lava flow," Betty said sadly.

"That's a pleasure you'll have to postpone for a spell, but there's a chore you could do for me, if you would."

"Of course. What is it?"

"Tell Natty Gordon I'll give myself up if he'll ride out here alone. Tell him I'll be at Round Butte this evening."

"I wouldn't trust Natty as far as I could throw his horse by his tail," Betty said doubtfully.

"He'll side with me after I explain things."

Betty stepped into the saddle and sat for a moment, staring at the pumice. "Any pumice I ever saw was sort of gray, Mack. How did they get that to look as dark as the lava?"

"Knowing the kind of brain Lou Kyle's got," Mack said, "I wouldn't try to guess." He ran his hand over the pumice. "Don't look like paint. Might be they rubbed it with charcoal or soot."

"What is pumice, Mack? Why is it different from any other lava?"

"Jimmy was telling me about it the last time I was out here. He had a hunk of it in his cabin. Said it was foam on a lava flow. Probably made when Round Butte exploded."

"Funny stuff," the girl said. She smiled at Mack and rode away.

Mack found a dry wash on the east side of the butte that

was deep enough to hide him and his sorrel. He slept most of the day, and in the late afternoon he built a small fire and cooked a meal. It was evening before he mounted and rode back to the other side of the butte. Leaving his sorrel behind a lava upthrust, he drew his gun and waited atop the lava until he saw Natty Gordon approaching. The deputy was riding slowly and cautiously, a Winchester carried across his saddle.

"Pull up, Natty," Mack said softly. "Don't start triggering, 'cause I've got a gun here in a mighty handy position."

Gordon pulled his horse to a stop, frightened eyes probing the dusk for a moment before he located Mack.

"That's fine," Mack said. "Now toss your Winchester down and likewise your Colt."

"You told Betty you'd give yourself up," Gordon complained.

"I aim to, but we've got talk to make first. You want me for stealing Tomahawk beef and killing Metolius Neele. That right?"

"That's right." Gordon dropped his Winchester and six-gun. "Mack, I know you're hell on tall red wheels. If you gave me an even break, I couldn't get you, but damn it, even your worst enemy says you'd keep a bargain."

"I told you I aimed to," Mack said, "but I'm not going back to town as long as Lou Kyle holds the whiphand like he does now."

"Don't make any difference about Kyle," Gordon said doggedly. "You've got to stand trial."

"I don't reckon so," Mack said sharply. "Let's lay out our cards. You're a politician who wants to hold a job. I want to get clear of these trumped-up charges against me. Likewise, I want to throw 'em back on Kyle where they belong. Now I claim it's smart for us to work together."

"Mebbeso," Gordon grunted, "but Soogan. . . ."

181

"Soogan's our man," Mack said quickly. "Right now, he won't stand for no talk against Kyle, but tonight you and me are gonna prove it's Kyle who stole his beef. Then Soogan will listen. In the long run, Natty, you'll be standing ace-high with everybody, including Soogan, because it ain't every deputy sheriff who can bring a crook like Kyle off his throne. Is it a deal?"

For a long moment Gordon stared at the bronze blob that was Mack's face. Finally he said: "I ain't never been one to gamble, Mack, but this is the time I will. It's a bargain."

"Pick up your weapons, mister." Mack rode around the lava and reined up beside Gordon. Quickly he sketched what had happened. He finished with: "Looks to me like the Carnes were in a position to do the stealing, and Kyle had the market with the railroad."

"That deal might have been rigged a long time ago," Gordon said thoughtfully. "You haven't seen Inky Blair for a while, have you?"

"No."

"He wrote to the head office of the Pioneer Valley Railroad about Yance Bishop, taking the contracts for horse feed and meat, without giving nobody else around here a chance. The upshot of it was the company sent their chief special agent into Axehandle to do a little nosing around."

"It's about ready to wind up, Natty. I'm thinking that last winter mebbe the Carnes punched a hole into the lava wall and fitted the pumice plug into it. You remember the long ridge that comes from his rim down to the floor of the cove?"

Gordon nodded. "I saw it the time we were down there."

"The way I've got it figgered that ridge takes off just about where this notch is. We'll wait till they open up the notch and nab the *hombre* who pulls the pumice out. Then we can take our look in the cove without having Soogan bellyaching about it and Dan Carne fixing to plug us."

"Guess I did a little bellyaching myself," Natty growled. "I don't like the notion of going down there, but I'll tag along."

They rode to the notch and dismounted. Mack whispered, "In case they don't open up, we'll lift the plug ourselves and go on down, but I'm guessing they'll open up."

The last red glow of a dying sun now left the sky, and darkness spilled out across the desert. The junipers made a scattering of sharply pointed blots, and the tang of sage was in the air. There was a brittle sharpness to the night noises that rode the high, thin air. Then there was the sound of boot heels on rock followed by the grinding of pumice on lava as the plug was lifted from its tight fit.

"I'll take him," Mack whispered.

Mack drew his gun and stood close to the notch, as the huge slab of pumice moved forward until it was clear of the wall and the man carrying it was beside Mack. The Carne man had no warning, and he made no sound when the gun barrel arced down upon his head. His arms broke free from around the pumice, and he sprawled limply forward. The pumice dropped to its base, teetered aimlessly for a time, and fell over on its side.

By the flare of a match flame Mack examined the fallen man. He said: "Stranger to me. You know him, Natty?"

"He's been around Axehandle," the deputy said grudgingly. "One of Kyle's men, I think."

While Mack bound and gagged the man, Gordon lifted the pumice plug and swore softly. "I wouldn't have believed that big a hunk of anything could be as light as it is, if I hadn't picked it up myself."

Mack had stepped into the V from which the pumice had been moved. He said: "Take a look at this, Natty. Don't it strike you they've blasted this wall out some way?"

Natty felt along the edges of the notch and moved on through the lava to the rim of the cove. "Yeah, looks like it. They must have put a charge of powder on this side. Reckon they wanted the side next to the desert to look plumb natural."

Mack thought of Jimmy Hinton, the only man who had lived within miles of the lava flow except the Carne brothers themselves. Apparently they had not feared him because he was a nester, a hog farmer, and a man from the outside. Yet Jimmy had discovered their secret, and he'd paid with his life for making that discovery. Mack said: "Come on, Natty."

The lava flow paralleled the edge of the rim, a bare thirty feet between them. Mack moved cautiously, finding the ridge that led to the cove floor broke off gently from the rim, but it was narrow and one false step to either side would send a man pinwheeling through space to his death.

"Take it easy, son," Gordon called softly. "I ain't got my wings."

Mack had stopped, his ears catching an unusual sound. "Natty, you hear anything?"

"Sounds like running water, but, hell, we're too far from the creek to hear it."

"It ain't the creek, Natty," Mack said. "I'm thinking we've found out how they got Soogan's beef." He moved on and came presently to a saucer-like hollow in the ridge top. The gurgle of water was unmistakable now, and a moment later he sloshed into it. "We should've brought our fishing poles."

"I'll be damned," Gordon breathed. He struck a match, its blaze shining across a pool of water. "They dug a hole through the lava wall, plugged it in the daytime with pumice, and took it out at night so Soogan's cows would drift through for a drink. That it, Mack?"

"That's the way I'd call it. Come on."

"Look, Mack." Natty stepped around the water and caught

up with Mack. "This is all neat and cute, but how did the Carne boys keep Soogan's cows all this time?"

"That's the thing we're gonna find out."

The ridge had widened, and the evidence that a large number of cattle had come along it was unmistakable. Half an hour later Mack and Gordon reached the floor of the cove not far from Pioneer Creek. They stood in silence for a time, ears keening the night air for human sounds. Far away a lamp in the Carne farmhouse made its pinpoint of light.

"You're still missing your ace," Gordon taunted, "and, if you don't turn it up, all this smart stuff you've discovered won't do no good."

"Which same would make you right happy," Mack murmured.

"No, it wouldn't," Gordon said slowly. "You've made a fool out of me more'n once, but things are shaping up a little different. While you was out of town, Inky Blair done some talking for you, and it kind of looks to me like folks around Axehandle have changed their minds about you. It's my guess that, if you stand trial, you'll find Kyle don't control the feeling around town like he did a week ago."

"Why?"

"Mebbe on account of this railroad agent who's in town. Those contracts had a smell about 'em that wasn't good. Then it might be folks just cotton to a gent who don't look at the odds before he starts fighting."

"Let's mosey." Mack went out on one of the boulders at the foot of the ridge and followed the edge of the grain field toward the haystack bulking darkly before them.

"We ain't gonna see anything in the dark," Gordon muttered. "Just now I hit my big toe on a rock and drove it plumb up into my knee. Darker'n the inside of a bull's belly at midnight."

Mack said nothing. Ahead of him were two wagons topped by hayracks. He thought of Dan Carne's load of hay he'd seen in town, and the water that dribbled from it. That, more than anything else in this fantastic pattern of robbery and murder, had puzzled him. The answer must be here. It had to be. He felt along the cliff until he was directly behind the haystack. Then the wall of the cliff broke sharply away from him. He struck a match and found a half dozen lanterns lined along the ground.

"What'n hell are those lanterns for?" Natty murmured. "I don't like this."

Mack lighted one of the lanterns and snapped the chimney down. "Looks to me like we're standing in the mouth of a cave."

"I don't want to do no cave exploring," Gordon shrilled. "Let's go back on top."

"We'll have a look first," Mack said grimly. He lifted the lantern above his head, its light making a yellow glare on the high roof. The walls, he judged, were fifty feet apart. Marks of wheels and horse hoofs in the dirt on the cave floor showed that wagons had gone in and out of the cave repeatedly.

"It's cold," Gordon said.

"A cave's always cold when it's warm outside. Grab a lantern so we'll have more light."

"I don't want a lantern," the deputy said, his teeth beginning to chatter. "Let's get out of here."

But Mack Jarvis had gone on into the cave, and now he made no move either to continue or to go back. Exultation poured through him in a great tide. The secret of the cove was no longer a secret. The light from his lantern showed long rows of beeves ahead of him hung in stiff precision from wooden racks. Below them a thick sheath of ice covered the floor.

Natty Gordon stood rigidly beside Mack. Neither spoke for a long moment, the paralysis of amazement holding them in a motionless silence. Then Mack said softly: "There it is, Natty. That's the ace you figgered I was missing. We're in a natural ice cave. They brought the cattle in, butchered 'em, and hung 'em up. They'd keep here till hell turned cold."

"Then they'd put 'em in a hayrack, cover 'em with hay, and haul 'em into Kyle's warehouse."

"That's my guess," Mack agreed. "What with the hay cover over 'em and some chunks of ice around 'em, they'd keep frozen for a long time. That water I saw coming out of the hay in town at Kyle's slaughterhouse must have been from the ice melting. Now I'm wondering why I didn't think of it before. Jimmy Hinton told me once he'd found a couple of ice caves back in the east Sundowns."

They went on into the cave, making their way over the precarious footing, Mack slapping at the frozen beeves and finding them rock solid. Ahead of him the row of beeves continued farther than Mack could see. The ice was thicker underfoot now, the floor tilting upward and making walking difficult.

"I'll take a steak," Gordon crowed, "cooked just like Betty Grant cooks 'em. Mack, let's take her one of these critters."

Mack held his lantern to the side of the cave, saw that it was solid ice, and that it was the same on the other side. "I'll bet they've cut this out," he said thoughtfully, "and used the ice to keep the meat frozen on the way into town."

"I heard some talk about the men getting sick at one camp. You reckon it might have spoiled?"

"Frozen meat spoils mighty soon after it thaws. If they got careless at one of the camps, and it spoiled, the boys would sure be unhappy." He looked back at Natty. "Dad Perrod told me he'd heard they were to get pork at one of the camps."

"I heard some such talk."

"Jimmy's hogs are gone," Mack went on. "Looks like they oughta be here."

"You'll see 'em if you go far enough, which you ain't." Dan Carne stepped into view ahead of Mack, a cocked Colt clutched in a hairy hand. Pete Carne was close behind, his grin wide and wicked. He jacked up the chimney of the dark lantern he carried, touched the wick with a match flame, and lowered the chimney.

Natty Gordon swore. Mack made no motion. The minute his hand started down, he'd die, so he waited, saying nothing, and watched the Carne brothers come down the sloping ice floor. Dan Carne's bulldog face held the triumphant look of a man who finally finds within his grasp the thing he most desires.

The Carnes stopped when they were within ten feet of Mack. Dan said: "You remember that time you saw me in town with a load of hay?"

"And stolen Tomahawk beef under the hay?"

"Yeah, that's right," Dan Carne said. "Only you and your star-packing friend didn't have sense enough to figger it out. I told you I had a hunch you'd be fool enough to come snooping around here again. I said that'd be the day. Remember?"

"I remember all right. What of it?"

"Why, nothing," Dan Carne said easily, "except that this is the day. This is the day you die."

Chapter Nineteen

Fear brought a gusty sigh out of Natty Gordon. Mack did not look back at him. They were trapped. There was no escaping that grim murder gun held in Dan Carne's hand.

"Go on," Pete Carne said testily. "Plug 'em. You're wasting time, Dan."

"We ain't in no real hurry," Dan said. "I want to tell Jarvis how big a fool he is. He acted about as smart, busting in here, as a kid on a snipe hunt. We heard you coming, so we dropped back into a corner in the cave, blew out our lantern, and waited."

"What were you doing back here at night?" Mack asked.

"Putting Hinton's hogs away. We figgered we'd have to hold 'em for a spell, until Kyle could pick up a few from some of the valley farmers."

"Who killed Jimmy?"

"Lou done it," Dan Carne said. "We caught Hinton up there on the ridge, watching us. When Lou came out that night, he said we couldn't take no chances, so we took Hinton back to the cabin and drilled him."

"Metolius?"

"We salivated him and Curly Isher. They got hard to handle, claimed they had a partnership coming. They had been plumb useful on account of they could nudge a few cows up to this end of the range, and nobody thought anything about it."

"What was the idea of packing Metolius over to Jimmy's cabin?"

"That was Lou's notion." Dan Carne chuckled. "Mighty tricky *hombre*, Lou is. He planted that gold button so you'd get wild enough to plug Soogan. We knew you'd be along purty soon, and you'd hightail for Tomahawk if you found the gold button. You'd tell Soogan about Metolius, and the Tomahawk boys would figger you done him in. Mighty near worked out, too, didn't it, Natty?"

"Now look, Dan . . . ," Gordon began.

"Aw, dry up," Dan Carne said contemptuously.

"Who put a slug along my noggin?" Mack asked.

"Lou again," Carne answered. "We aimed to keep an eye on the cabin, figgering you'd show up. If Soogan's boys didn't get you, we would. We didn't know about that *dinero* Hinton had in the bank. That's gonna come in plumb handy to Lou. He's got himself spread out so much he's about to lose his shirt. Fact is, he'd never have got into this cow steal with us if he hadn't had to have some quick cash."

"How much did Jimmy leave?"

"Twenty-five thousand in a box in the Axehandle bank, and Lou's got the key. Kind of foolish the way Hinton did that business." Dan Carne prodded his brother with an elbow and snickered. "I'll bet he's turning over in his grave right now."

"Why didn't Kyle finish me?"

"Lou was plumb skittish. He's been afraid all along somebody was gonna get onto him being in this business. He claims he don't want nothing now but to get out and keep his reputation. Says he wants to marry Rosella and run Tomahawk soon as Soogan kicks the bucket." Dan snickered again. "I'll dance at their wedding, just like I said, Jarvis, but you won't."

"I still don't know why Kyle didn't finish me," Mack said doggedly.

"Somebody opened up on me, and he got scared. I was outside on my bronc'. Lou was in the cabin. He got the key and Hinton's letter. When he heard the shooting, he came out of there like he was sliding downhill into hell. He figgered it was some of the Tomahawk boys, and he didn't want Soogan to get the idea he knew what was going on."

"Come on," Pete Carne said. "I'm getting cold. Plug 'em. Go on. Plug 'em. We'll throw 'em into the hole and go to bed."

"Might as well," Dan agreed. "Don't make any difference now how much they know. Reckon I'm wasting my time."

"You know how a cave like this happens to have ice in it?" Mack asked.

"We don't care," Pete Carne snarled. "It's here, and that's good enough for us."

"Shut up, Pete," Dan said coolly. "I kind of like to hear Jarvis talk. He's always been so damned tough, and he's had the devil's own luck. It does me good to see him stall around to get a few minutes more to live. You sure hate the notion of dying, don't you, Jarvis?"

"I don't want to die before I finish one more chore, Dan. Now this business about the ice being here is plumb interesting. When you killed Jimmy Hinton, you killed the smartest *hombre* this range ever saw. He told me about these ice caves. They don't have cracks in the lava floor so the water can leak away. He said the freezing weather lasted a long time at this altitude. The cold air circulates around through the rock, and water that dribbles in freezes. Mebbe from that spring up on the ridge. Of course, the air warms up in summer, but not enough in some places to overtake the cold air in winter. Jimmy said it was a lagging effect in the change of temperature. He talked like a book sometimes. He was. . . ."

"Damn it, Dan, I'm gonna . . . ," Pete Carne began and reached for his Colt.

This was the moment. There would not be another. The lantern glow, falling upon the Carne men, showed the wicked set of their faces, the way vicious hatred marred their features. The memory of Cat Carne's death at Mack Jarvis's hand was running its red-hot prod through their minds. Dan Carne

191

called: "It's my job, Pete."

Mack had been standing between two of the frozen beeves. Now, gauging carefully the moment Dan Carne was going to fire, Mack threw himself sideways. His feet spilled out from under him, and he fell belly flat on the ice. Dan Carne's gun thundered, the sound of it, caught in the narrow confines of the cave, was thrown back in a series of prolonged echoes. Then Mack's gun added its roar to the long racket of Carne's shot. He had drawn as he'd fallen, and he'd slid back along the sloping ice so that one of the low-hung beeves had for the moment partially hidden him from Dan Carne. Carne, stepping forward, came directly into Mack's view. Mack, lying flat on the ice, laced a bullet into his heart.

Pete Carne had jerked his gun the instant Dan fired. Both of them were ignoring Natty Gordon and watching Mack. Natty, taking advantage of that short moment of inattention, plucked his gun and pulled the trigger just as Pete Carne became aware of his motion and swung to cover him. The shot caught Pete in the knee, knocking him off his feet. He came sliding and rolling toward Mack, cursing and trying to bring his gun into action, and not being able to do so.

"Don't shoot him, Natty," Mack called.

"Why not, damn him?" Gordon shouted. "He'd have drilled us soon enough."

Pete had come to a stop a few feet from Mack. He rolled over on his belly, raising his head and his arm for another shot. It was then Mack sledged him across the head with the barrel of his gun, knocking him out.

"Why not finish him?" Natty Gordon asked angrily.

"I'd judge Dan's dead, the way he went down," Mack answered. "Pete's the kind of huckleberry who'll talk. It's your job to get it out of him."

Natty had a look at Dan Carne and came to stand beside

Mack. "Dan's dead all right, and I'll make Pete talk if I have to shoot his other leg off." He cleared his throat and blurted: "Damn it, Mack, I sure have backed the wrong horse. There's been a few times when I've had my doubts, but it just didn't add up for a man in Kyle's position to be in this kind of a mess. Anyhow, I wasn't smart enough to see through it the way they had the play rigged."

"We ain't done," Mack said soberly.

"I know," Gordon said, "and we'll get Kyle. Then we'll tell Soogan a few things. I . . . I . . . , well, damn it, I'm sorry I ain't smarter'n I am, Mack."

Gordon held out his hand, and Mack took it. He said: "Let's get Pete out of here."

Outside a man raised a cry: "What's going on, Dan?"

Mack whirled, caught a faint figure in the mouth of the cave, and drove a bullet at him. The man made no answering fire. He faded into the night, and Mack, running after him, could not get his eyes on him again. A moment later Mack heard the pound of a horse's hoofs. He said soberly: "We may have trouble finding Kyle now, Natty."

Mack found two saddle horses tied at the end of the hay-stack. He patched up Pete Carne's knee and tied him into the saddle. Then he and Gordon mounted the other horse and, leading Pete's mount, rode along the ridge to the rim and through the notch in the lava flow. They tied the man Mack had knocked cold into the saddle of the horse Mack and Gordon had been riding and, mounting their own horses, took the trail for Axehandle.

It was well past midnight when they rode along Axehandle's dark, main street and locked a cell door on their prisoners. Mack said: "You'd better get Doc, Natty. Pete's knee is pretty bad."

"What are you going to do?"

"See if Kyle's home."

"That's my job, too," Natty said sharply.

"You're the law. I'm just a jigger with a personal problem I aim to work out with Kyle. You go get the doc." Mack swung into the saddle again and rode around the block and along the side street to Kyle's home.

There were no lights in the windows. Night's quiet lay all around. Mack palmed his gun and moved silently up the path. Kyle would be warned by the man who had seen them in the cave, and he'd know his empire had been pulled down around his ears, but whether he was a man to stay and fight was something Mack doubted. The front door was unlocked. Mack stepped in and went along the hall to Kyle's bedroom. It was empty. Mack lighted a lamp and saw the evidence of flight.

Mack rode back to Main Street and left his horse in the stable. He didn't know how utterly weary he was until he reeled into his room in the back of his feed store building and sank down upon his bed. Dad Perrod was not around. He was, Mack guessed, staying with Betty.

It was late afternoon when Mack awoke. The first thing he saw was Inky Blair, sitting beside the bed, his feet cocked up on the foot of it, a half-smoked cigar tucked into one corner of his mouth. He said: "Son, if you hadn't waked up pretty *pronto*, I was aiming to ride out to the cove and get me a nice hunk of ice to lay right on top of your belly."

Mack swung his feet to the floor, knuckled the sleep from his eyes, and shook his head. "I don't think I ever slept in my life before, Inky."

"Twelve hours or more you've been pounding that pillow." Inky took a new bite on his cigar. "Betty's got a meal fixed up. Just you and me and her and Dad. There's hot water on the stove. Get up and start axing that sagebrush off your face."

194

While Mack shaved and dressed, Inky told him that the news was all over town, that Kyle and Tash Terris had disappeared, and that Natty Gordon had a signed statement from Pete Carne giving a complete account of what had happened from the moment Kyle and the Carne brothers first made their agreement.

"Whatever Natty didn't get out of Pete," Inky said, "he got in their house. He took some of the boys and rode out there this morning. There were three hay hands around, but they didn't make any trouble, and neither did Kyle's men here in town. Seems that Kyle owed them back wages, and they aren't thinking much good about him. Fact is, Kyle was getting pretty shaky all around. And we had him pegged for a rich galoot." Inky laughed. "So did Soogan."

"Where is Soogan?"

"He's down at the Casino right now. So is George Queen. They had a look in the ice cave, and Soogan's eyes are still bugged halfway out of his head. They didn't find many hides. It seems there's a hole just off to the right of where you went into the ice cave. Sort of a fissure that goes halfway to hell, the way they tell it. Anyhow, the Carnes tossed the hides and offal into that hole. They figured the hides were the kind of evidence they didn't want around, but those hides wouldn't have made any difference. Not after Pete's confession."

Mack cleaned his gun, loaded it, and slid it into the holster. He said: "Tell Betty I'll be over there in a minute."

"Where are you going?" Inky demanded.

"Walking," Mack said and left the feed store.

Someone saw him and raised a shout. They came out of the stores and business places, wanting to shake his hand and slap him on the back. This was not Lou Kyle's town now, Mack saw, and yet these were the same men who only a few days before had bowed and scraped in front of Kyle and called

Mack a tough hand they could do without. Mack pushed his way on through them, his face a granite mask, and went into the Casino.

Natty Gordon was inside. So, too, were Soogan and George Queen and most of the Tomahawk men. Natty called jubilantly: "There he is, gents. The jasper with the devil's own luck, or so Dan Carne said. About a couple of shakes later Dan was down in hell hobnobbing with the devil himself at Mack's request."

Mack thought fleetingly of that time only a few days ago when he and Inky had stood in this same saloon and listened to Lou Kyle make his proud announcements. They were days that seemed months. The weariness of those days was still in him, the smell of the powder smoke and blood in his nostrils, the sight of men sprawling in death before his eyes. They had been familiar smells and sights in his tumbleweed years, but he had thought they were behind him. He had bargained for a home and a community in which to settle down, and most of all he had bargained for the love of a girl. Lou Kyle was smashed. That much Mack had done, but the things he had bargained for were the important things, and he had not achieved them.

Mack came along the bar to where Soogan stood. The old man pulled at his mustache, and he looked abashed. He blurted: "Hod dang it, son, I sure do hate to take a licking, and I hate to say I've been wrong, but I'm taking a licking right now and telling you I'm so damned ashamed of myself I could crawl under an angleworm's belly and not even touch the top of this here bonnet I'm wearing."

"But you wouldn't believe Kyle had his hand in your cattle disappearing, and you gave your boys orders to smoke me down."

"I'm a stubborn, bone-headed fool," Soogan Wade admitted, "and I'm sure glad you got clear that night." Then his eyes narrowed. "Seems like I'm remembering something about you suckering around after one of Lou's smart tricks, too. You figgered I beefed Hinton when you found that gold button."

A quick grin cracked Mack's face and was gone. "Seems like I remember something about that."

"Mebbe you feel like shaking?" Soogan asked hesitantly and held out a hand.

Mack took it, and gripped it, feeling the old man's inherent honesty and regret for the mistakes that had been made. Wade pulled a roll of bills out of his pocket and handed them to Mack. He said: "Five hundred dollars, son. That was our deal. I dunno what good that frozen beef is gonna do me, but mebbe I can keep on selling it to the railroad. I won't get what Lou was getting, though. He was making himself some real money out of that. Getting about three prices the way I hear it."

Mack had swung to face Queen. When he spoke, his voice crackled across the space between them with the venomous quality of a snapping blacksnake. "George, I'm remembering how you aimed to hang Jimmy Hinton. Likewise I'm remembering how you claimed that Jimmy stole the cows, and that I was in it. Likewise, again, you were talking, that night I was at Tomahawk, about it being a pleasure to smoke me down. I guess mebbe this is as good a place as any to make your try."

But George Queen had no stomach for it. He looked at Soogan Wade, his eyes narrowed and hard, his great pride slowly coming out of him. He said: "You're hard on a man, Mack. You've got no call to make this play."

"Plenty of call the way I see it. You let Curly Isher and Metolius Neele pull the wool over your eyes. You've got a one-inch brain that had room for the notion Jimmy and I were to blame, and then you didn't have no room for anything else. You're no ramrod, mister. You'll ruin Soogan, if you hang on there long enough. Now, play your hand the way you see it."

Again Queen laid his eyes on Soogan's face, a long, searching look that seemed to tell him what he wanted to know. He wheeled and went out, and presently the sound of his fast-running horse came to the men in the Casino.

"Looks like I need a ramrod, Mack," Soogan said. "Want the job?"

"No," Mack said, and left the saloon.

Chapter Twenty

The woman who had come from Minter City to help Betty was in the restaurant when Mack came in. "Betty's in her living room," she said, and Mack went on through the back and made the turn into the living room.

Betty was standing beside the table, waiting for him. Mack, looking at her, felt the sweetness that was in her, the loveliness, the gallant womanliness that asked nothing of life except to be her own person and return a man's love who was worthy of it.

Inky Blair said: "About time you showed up."

"Sure is." Dad Perrod stepped over to the window, opened it, and tossed a quid of tobacco outside. "My tapeworm's been rearing up his head and bellering to beat all hell the last half hour."

There was little talk while they ate. Betty had cooked steak and onions, and the bottle of ketchup was beside Mack's plate. When they were done, Betty brought in the dried apple pie and filled their coffee cups.

Inky Blair picked up the sugar bowl and eyed it disapprovingly. "Funny thing, Betty," he said. "I can't understand it. When we sat down, this thing was full. Now it's empty. Must have a hole in the bottom."

Mack did not make his usual cutting remark when Betty left to fill the sugar bowl. He sat slackly in his chair, the long tension gone out of him for a moment. He felt like a man who had been in a high wind and just now had come into the quiet.

"What are your plans, Mack?" Betty asked.

"I don't have any," he said. He had looked around the room, noting that Rosella's wedding dress was not in sight. "I guess there's no hurry about making up my mind."

"I said you couldn't do your fighting alone," Betty murmured, "but I guess you did. We weren't of much help."

"You were a lot of help," Mack said quickly. "All of you, but you most of all, Betty. Had it not been for you, Kyle would surely have killed me." He looked at them: fat-cheeked Inky Blair, gnarled, grizzled Dad Perrod, and Betty. He felt the close ties that bound them. The wildness and the fury of the past weeks had made those ties, and nothing that lay ahead could change them.

"Why, thank you, friend," Inky said. "I'll take all the credit you want to pass out."

"It would have been everything," Mack said slowly, "if Jimmy could have been here."

"That's right," Inky nodded.

"I hope he knows how it's worked out," Mack went on.

"I'm sure he does," Betty said.

"Funny about Kyle." Dad Perrod scooted back his chair and reached into a pocket for his plug of tobacco. "I didn't think he'd run like this."

"I wonder if he has," Betty said thoughtfully.

"Sure he has," Inky grunted. "He didn't have any choice. He was into trouble up to his neck, and he knew he couldn't pull it through."

Mack stood up. "Thanks for the meal, Betty. I can't recollect offhand of any grub that tasted so good." He went out quickly, and, as he left the restaurant, he saw that the stage was standing in front of the hotel. In a few minutes it would roll out over the valley road toward Minter City and go on to the Columbia. If he were done here, he thought, he'd take that stage.

"Mack." It was Rosella, coming along the walk behind him. When he turned, she came on to him. "I'm glad you're all right, Mack. I was worried after you left Tomahawk the other night."

"I made out." He looked at her, a tall girl beside him, perfectly poised and sure of herself, and feeling that this man was hers, that she had never really lost him. She was here, within reach of him, and she would not be marrying Lou Kyle. This thought rushed through his mind, and he was startled by it, but it brought him no pleasure. He had made his dreams about this girl, and they were gone.

"I hear that Jimmy Hinton left you a lot of money," Rosella said.

"I don't have it. I guess Kyle got it out of the bank box and pulled out with it."

"You'll get it back," she said confidently. "What will you do?"

"I thought I'd mebbe build a hospital. Jimmy would like the notion, and this will be a big town. It'll need a hospital."

"Don't be a fool," Rosella said sharply. "There are a dozen opportunities here in front of you that would make you rich."

"Might be." Mack turned away and moved toward the stable.

"Mack." Rosella ran after him, caught his arm, and brought him around to face her. "Don't you understand?" She held up her left hand. There was no ring on her third finger.

"Yes," he said slowly, "I understand." This time, when he walked away, she did not come after him.

Inky Blair overtook Mack by the time he reached the stable. "You and Rosella," he said heatedly. "You crazy, blind, damned fool. Betty's sold out, and she's taking the stage. You didn't even say good bye."

Mack went past Inky toward the stall that held his sorrel. "I'm taking a ride to Trumpet," he said, only half hearing what Inky had said and not even knowing that Inky had gone on along the street to the hotel. "Kyle ain't one to run far, and that's about. . . ."

"No," Kyle said, "you don't have to ride to Trumpet. Step into that stall, Jarvis."

As Mack moved into the empty stall, he raised his eyes to the hole in the loft. Lou Kyle was lying on the floor, only his head and hand showing. In that hand was a cocked .45. There was a stirring in the stall beside Mack, and Tash Terris came and stood beside him.

The hosteler was gone. Inky Blair wasn't in sight. This was it. The job had been done, but Mack Jarvis would not live to see what came of it.

Kyle said tonelessly: "Your luck's run out, Jarvis. It couldn't go on like it's been running. You didn't expect that, did you?"

Mack held his answer for a moment. Terris was close behind him, panting like a great dog at the end of a chase. Mack could picture his huge hands, fingers splayed, ready to break his neck. He heard the giant breathe. "Want I should give it to him now, Boss?"

"Just a minute, Tash. I want Jarvis to know he isn't winning the big pot. I told him I'd rake it in. That's what I'm doing. I was busted here. Got into too many things, and lost my head in a poker game in The Dalles that damned near finished me. I might have pulled out by marrying Rosella, but I couldn't pull it off soon enough, and the beef money was coming in too slow. Now I'm going out of here with a nice chunk of cash, Jarvis. Hinton's money, which he conveniently left in a bank box. What do you think of that for a pat hand, friend?"

"You've got the *dinero* on you?"

"You bet I have, and nobody's going to stop us from getting out of here with it. Tash don't make no racket when he twists a man's neck. We'll haul your carcass up here beside the hosteler's. When it gets dark, we'll pick up our horses and head for Trumpet, just like you guessed."

Kyle paused, and by the thin light from the window behind Mack, he could see visible evidence of the hate that washed through the big man, had corroded his soul, and left its mark upon his face. He had sacrificed the hours that would probably have meant freedom to kill this man who had brought him down.

"You probably left your horse here when you got back from the cove," Kyle went on, "but we didn't get here in time to catch you. I knew you'd be back before long, so we waited. Tash could have finished you the minute you stepped into that stall, but I wanted you to know. I've made some mistakes, Jarvis, most of them underestimating you. I set up the play in the Casino when I told you about Rosella, so you'd tackle me, and Tash would have a chance to snap your neck. You were too smart, and after that nothing went right. Not till this time. All right, Tash."

Whatever move Mack made meant death for him. Tash Terris stood behind him, bottling him up so that he couldn't make a run for the door. If he tried, or if he went for his gun, he'd draw a slug from Lou Kyle's .45.

There was this one, short moment while he groped blindly, and his thoughts came back to him with no good in them. *This was it.* Yet, even as his mind gripped that fatal conclusion, a great bellow of pain rolled out of Tash Terris. Mack acted without looking around. He pulled his gun, throwing himself against the wall of the stall as he brought the Colt up.

Kyle's attention had been diverted for a short interval of time by Terris's cry. It was long enough. He fired once at Mack, a quick shot before he caught the change of Mack's position, and missed. Hard on the heels of that explosion came the thunder of Mack's gun. Kyle came out of the loft, plunging through the hole and turning over once in the air before he fell into a manger, a broken, lifeless body.

Mack wheeled, caught the picture in one quick glance. Inky Blair had a pitchfork in his hands and was running it at Terris's legs, but the giant was plunging at Inky, the prick of those shiny prongs not enough to stop him. His hands were closing around Inky's neck when Mack shot him through the head. Terris fell into the litter of the runway without knowing what had hit him.

Inky sank back against the wall, eyes wide with fright. "Say, you just got him in time, pardner," he gasped. "I could feel my tonsils beginning to bulge before he ever laid a hand on me." Then he grinned. "You should have seen him jump when I got him. I got him good. Right square in the seat of his pants."

"Thanks," Mack said simply. "Betty was sure right when she said I couldn't do it all alone."

The thunder of the stage, crossing the plank bridge over the creek, came to him then, and with it the stabbing realization that Betty Grant was leaving Axehandle, that she was going out of his life, and with it was the full knowledge of what she meant to him.

"Get that money off of Kyle, Inky," Mack said as he threw gear on his sorrel. Men poured into the stable, Dad Perrod among them, and Mack called to him: "Dad, pick up my sorrel."

Mack was in the saddle, then, and pouring steel to his horse. He roared across the bridge and a moment later came alongside the stage. "Pull up," he yelled.

The driver looked down in amazement and then yanked on the lines. "This a holdup, Mack?" he asked.

"No. Just taking on a passenger." Mack stepped down and took his seat beside Betty. He called: "Let her roll."

There were only the two of them in the stage. For a moment

they looked at each other. Then Betty murmured, "Hello. You going somewhere?"

"Are you?"

"I'm going to Minter City."

"It's a good town for a honeymoon," Mack said softly, "but we'll be back. We've got to help Inky Blair build a town."

He kissed her then, holding her hard against him, the soft sweetness of her lips building a fire that ran in a swift and torrid stream through him. There was this moment that brought him to a place where he had never been before, a place where reality held everything that had ever been in his dreams. It was this for which he had fought, this for which he had lived.

She lay inside his arm, her face upturned to his, and her smile was a glorious and beautiful thing that only Mack Jarvis would see. She whispered. "My dear, I thought you'd never know."

Wayne D. Overholser has won three Golden Spur awards from the Western Writers of America and has a long list of fine Western titles to his credit. He was born in Pomeroy, Washington, and attended the University of Montana, University of Oregon, and the University of Southern California before becoming a public school teacher and principal in various Oregon communities. He began writing for Western pulp magazines in 1936 and within a couple of years was a regular contributor to Street & Smith's *Western Story* and Fiction House's *Lariat Story Magazine*. *Buckaroo's Code* (1948) was his first Western novel and remains one of his best. In the 1950s and 1960s, having retired from academic work to concentrate on writing, he would publish as many as four books a year under his own name or a pseudonym, most prominently as Joseph Wayne. *The Bitter Night*, *The Lone Deputy*, and *The Violent Land* are among the finest of the early Overholser titles. He was asked by William MacLeod Raine, that dean among Western writers, to complete his last novel after Raine's death. Some of Overholser's most rewarding novels were actually collaborations with other Western writers: *Colorado Gold* with Chad Merriman and *Showdown at Stony Creek* with Lewis B. Patten. Overholser's Western novels, no matter under what name they have been published, are based on a solid knowledge of the history and customs of the American frontier West, particularly when set in his two favorite Western states, Oregon and Colorado. When it comes to his characters, he writes with skill, an uncommon sensitivity, and a consistently vivid and accurate vision of a way of life unique in human history.